Jacks
&
Hands

A Novel By

Wig Nelson

WIG NELSON

ISBN-10 0983314438
ISBN-13 9780983314431

Printed in the United States of America.

This Book is dedicated to all the lawyers in the world who became lawyers for the wrong reason. The men and women who continue to exploit the vulnerable positions of their fellow man for the same reason why we climb mountains: because they are there.

Cover art designed by
WranglerRoy Images
Carrollton, VA

Xeries Press
Indialantic, Florida
XP Publishing

Acknowledgments

I don't think I really want to mention anyone in the front of this book. I would be highly insulted if anyone mentioned me on an acknowledgment page of a book like this. Unless, of course, if my name was Satan or Lucifer. Then I would be very pleased.

To be honest, I'm a little disappointed that my name is on the cover. Some people have told me that there is no such thing as evil or sin. They are wrong. I have been told that sin is merely the fact that some people miss the mark.

This is a story about a man who misses the mark in a very big way. I suppose if I am to acknowledge anyone besides Satan for inspiring this work, I should thank all of us for having a dark side. I imagine the nature of man is both good and bad for a number of reasons, and we shall forever remain the victims of ourselves

Also by Wig Nelson

The Sirens Trilogy*

Sirens*

The First Church of Siren*

Online*

The Psychic

Starry Night

The Conga Player's Dues

String Theory and the Transparent Patient

The Little Shop of Lyrics

The Monster

Jacks
&
Hands

A Novel By

Wig Nelson

Prologue

Melissa Coolidge stood outside Jackson Hand's front entrance and wiped a tear from her eye. She pinched her breasts at the nipples to make them perk up and then rang the doorbell. Jackson Hand opened the door and ushered her in while talking with his advertising agency on a cordless phone. On the other end of the line were a guitarist and three singers performing the *Jacks and Hands* jingle,

Helping Hands - gifted Hands –
Jacks and Hands can help you.
Helping Hands - gifted Hands
are just a call away.

Hand led Melissa to his living room and placed her in the middle of the room with her arms at her sides. He slowly walked around her studying the curves of her body as he continued to listen to the jingle,

Helping Hands – loving Hands –
Jacks and Hands can help you.
Helping Hands – gifted hands

are just a call away.
They'll clean your home – so you can go out playing.

They'll do the laundry – and put the clothes away.
They'll feed your loved ones – any meal you say.
Gifted Hands are just a call away.

Hand then motioned for Melissa to take off her shirt with the Hands logo embroidered on the breast. He studied her for a moment and then motioned for her to remove her white pants and panties. He continued to walk slowly around her as he listened to the rest of the jingle,

Helping hands – gifted Hands –
Jacks and Hands can help you.
Helping hands – gifted Hands
are just a call away.
They'll do your yard work while you're at your office.
They'll do your shopping and put the food away.
They'll paint your bathroom–living room– any room you say.
Gifted Hands are just a call away.

Hand then spoke into the phone, "That's fine. Make sure to run it during drive time. I want people rushing around realizing that there isn't enough time in the day to get everything done and that they need a Hand." He broke the connection without even saying good-bye. Melissa stood naked before him trying not to cry. He asked her, "How is your father, Melissa?"

A tear escaped her eye and rolled down her cheek. She wiped it with the back of her hand and said, "He's still alive. That's why I'm here, naturally."

"You're a good daughter, Melissa," said Hand. He then motioned for her to kneel in front of him and said, "Now, let's see how good you really are."

~

Jackson Hand lived in the tallest condominium he could find. That was his only criteria. He merely wanted to be above everyone else physically. He spent his life looking up at people from his five-foot-six frame and simply had enough of it. It didn't matter how tall his neighbors were. If he occupied the penthouse, he would be above them.

He built an empire from a modest beginning by daring to be criminal. It was the only promise of a chance worth risking. Hard work can blow up in your face. You can work for years and then a change in the law or licensing requirements can undo a decade of dreams. Not to mention the insurance requirements to have a staff of reasonably paid employees.   There was no way.   In order to pay his employees a decent wage, he had to exploit the incriminating efforts of some of them. He called them his *stable* and there were twelve of them. They were five men and seven women who enticed their unwitting customers into sexual situations to gain an unfair advantage. But unfair was relative. He only preyed on the rich. He justified his actions by making the assumption that his targets could only enjoy their position by exploiting an unfair advantage of their own.

Mr. Hand was a dealer of despair, purveyor of piteousness and a master of malevolence. He was excited by the dirty deeds of his design - the dirtier the better and the greater the excitement.

Violence had little place in the panorama of his perilous pallet. His size had always governed his actions to be more than amiable physically. Mr. Hand never found himself personally in a fight; however, his minions were responsible for many lives damaged in the name of monetary gain. Lives lost as well if the truth should come to light. A God of retribution would lament the fact that Mr. Hand had only one life to be taken in order to balance out his soul, hopefully, to be taken in a very ugly way. Many people shared this as their mantra.

Jackson Hand began his empire with a simple premise. There will always be a need for service industry.

Water heaters always fail in time. A home is in constant need of cosmetic attention and certainly never more so than at a time just prior to a sale. You can live with your old kitchen cabinets while you enjoy the fact that your house is yours to live in, but at the time of a sale, certain upgrades are a necessity. Donald Trump once said that the definition of a loser is a guy who's selling his car and doesn't bother to wash it.

Jackson Hand made sure those words were never lost on him. That was the essence of his business. He provided quality work from quality craftsmen. No one worked for *Jacks and Hands* unless he was proficient in all the trades. They were the best of the best. The closest scrutiny wouldn't find a nail in the crown molding above a set of kitchen cabinets. The copper connections to a water heater not only had clean sweat fittings, but they also were sanded with an emery cloth and briefly lacquered as well. Everything shined with a promise of perfection when a Jack was through with his task.

And then there were the Hands. A Hand was a truly talented individual as well. The privileged few who could afford a Hand were treated to a gourmet chef, an efficient household organizer, a price conscious shopper, as well as a tutor for their children and a laundress and seamstress.

The Hands weren't cheap. At sixty dollars per hour with a four-hour minimum the Jacks and Hands weren't for everyone. Only the top three percent of the general population ever considered hiring them. For those people the cost was never a consideration. The Hands ingratiated themselves to their employer's families in a number of ways. They would pick up the kids from school, feed them a snack, drive them to soccer or dance recitals, and shop for groceries to prepare dinner for them when they were picked up a short time later. They learned how the families liked their food prepared and made sure that they were pleased with their performance. They helped with homework and science projects as well as term papers.

The Jacks made themselves useful where the young boys were concerned. They would instruct them how to throw a football or "stick" an approach shot with a pitching wedge close to a short-sided pin placement. Many of their customers' homes had putting greens in the back yard, which was a convenient venue for teaching the finer points of the short game. They became friends. They became indispensable. They became the weapons of Jackson Hand to bring down the best of families. Each of them was honed sharp with respect to their duties, as sharp as the tines of the devil's pitchfork and just as consequential. They were weapons for a small man with a smaller heart and the largest of agendas. They preyed on the weaknesses of their tragic dependents. They pitied them for their weakness and were grateful for its providence. The Jacks and Hands were put in a position to take advantage of those who wrote the book on taking advantage of others. They were houses that were built on sorrows of the innocent and their misdirected trust. Cruel laughter echoing through empty marble hallways. Notches on a bankbook. Feathers in a cap.

Some accounts were cancelled for lack of opportunity. Some people had no weakness to exploit. It was quickly determined whether there was fertile ground to plant the seeds of deception. A lonely woman wears a message on her brow. A Jack can read the volume of her regrets. When a lonely man sends indiscretion across his lips, a Hand is soon to have the upper hand. Thus the true tools of lust are embraced for their utility. The weakness of humanity easily falls prey to its lost promise of equality. The prom you were never asked to. The passion that life must forfeit for lack of the privilege to fail.

But the Hands were there for the taking. The Jacks were there as well. What was believed to be a bargain became a living hell. What was perceived to be a harmless dance was purgatory for those who fell.

When any member of the family engaged in a sexual activity with a Jack or a Hand, the room was examined for the feasibility of future hidden video devices. Usually, an air conditioner return vent or register became a convenient location to set up surveillance equipment. When the family was away for at least thirty minutes, a highly skilled Jack would facilitate the installation. Then the Jack or Hand would activate the camera on a future occasion and initiate the sexual encounter. The blackmail letter was always soon to follow.

The Jacks and Hands had very strict uniforms. The Jacks wore white shirts and overalls and drove white Ford F-150 pick-up trucks. The Hands wore white shirts with the embroidered symbol of the two hands crossed at the wrists and thumbs to create a suggestion of a dove in flight. They also wore white pants and white sox and sneakers. The hands drove white Toyota Camrys. All of the vehicles were supplied by Jackson Hand. He could well afford it. He was collecting nearly one hundred-twenty-thousand dollars a month in blackmail revenue. The Jacks and Hands were all attractive people with trim waistlines and fair complexions. They exuded an air of sexuality; however, they were required to always wear modest clothing and maintain an outward appearance of propriety. The only exception was when a Hand from his stable was ordered to perform a sexual favor in his penthouse.

Chapter One

J ay West had been a Jack for about a year and a half when he met a Hand that was recently hired named Nellie Brighton. Jay was a strong, young twenty-three-year-old man with light blond hair and a slight mustache. His eyebrows were curved and bushy, which gave the impression that his eyes were smiling. His strong six-foot frame spoke of long hours of determined conditioning, though he carried himself with the grace of a dancer.

Nellie was a beautiful nineteen-year-old with short brown hair and striking dark eyes. She had full sensuous lips and projected an air of adventurous sexuality. Her trim figure spoke of a commitment to muscle tone that many a runway model fell hopelessly short of. Rather than the angular look of the emaciated waif, her body took on the gently rounded suggestion of pure womanhood.

She had completed her freshman year at the University of Central Florida, but her college career was interrupted by a drug conviction. She was innocent of charges against her but was destined to go to prison anyway. She had no choice but to spend the college money that her family had saved for her on a defense attorney and a plea bargain.

The only real mistake she made was in choosing the wrong defense attorney. She had to learn the hard way that he was much more of a criminal than the people he represented. After her conviction she was headed for Crawford Women's Prison where death could be dealt at every turn of the indifferently watchful eyes of the correction officers. Crawford was a hell-hole and Nellie was well on her way to it.

The circumstances that led to her arrest were a constant reminder that it was a cruel world out there with everyone scratching and clawing just to survive. She was in a nightclub that had a reputation for selling narcotics. The drugs held no attraction for her - she was merely there to meet a girl named Sheila who was a friend of her brother's girlfriend Bobbie. Sheila was supposedly interested in attending the University of Central Florida in Orlando, and Nellie told Bobbie that she would talk to Sheila and give her some advice about housing and applying for a student loan. The nightclub was raided when the two women were in the bathroom together. When the police entered the bathroom, Nellie's confiscated purse proved to contain a considerable number of Ecstasy tablets individually wrapped for sale.

Her defense attorney's name was Brian Sorell, and he promised her a light sentence provided she could produce ten thousand dollars. He claimed that the plea bargain was only feasible with a payoff to the prosecutor's office *"in cash after dark."*

As it later turned out, she was given six months at Crawford and two years probation. She did almost five months before being part of an early release program due to overcrowding at the prison. Upon her release, and subsequent assignment to a probation officer, Sorrell contacted her with the promise of a job interview.

She applied at Jacks and Hands the next day. The interview with Jackson Hand was brief but successful. Hand informed her that he was well aware of her *"recent run-in with the law."* He told her that a drug test was mandatory every six months in order to be employed by Jacks and Hands. She assured Mr. Hand that that would never be a problem. She never did drugs. He said to her, "Well, you have a police record that states otherwise."

"I swear to you Mr. Hand that the drugs they found in my purse weren't mine."

"Then you were just holding them for someone. A friend perhaps?" he asked.

"No, that wasn't it," she assured him. "Someone put them in my purse. Probably when I was washing my hands."

"Uh huh," said Hand doubtfully.

"I'm telling you the truth," she argued.

"Look, Ms. Brighton, you have the job. I'm willing to put your past behind you," he said.

"My past?" she questioned. "There's nothing wrong with my past."

"You were in prison, Ms. Brighton. We're not in the habit of hiring ex-cons. Can you assure me that your drug use has come to an end?"

"But you don . . ."

"Yes, or no, Ms. Brighton," he demanded. *"Yes, or No?"*

She knew the money was too good to pass up. After the company took their cut, it worked out to forty-five dollars an hour.

"Yes," she said weakly.

"That's a good girl," said Hand. "I'm willing to give you a six-month trial period at three-quarter's pay."

"Three-quarter's?" she protested.

"Take it or leave it, Ms. Brighton. I have a busy day ahead of me."

"I'll take it," she said.

Hand was pleased with his new acquisition. Nellie Brighton was a true beauty and only nineteen years old. She was a fine addition to his *stable*. It was an attractive collection of weapons to use against the weaknesses of society. Sorell was right. She was worth every penny of the two thousand dollars that he paid him for her. He told her

12

where to report the next morning in order to begin her training. She was to purchase a pair of white Reebok Cross Trainers from the local Dillard's at the mall. They would give her a twenty-five percent discount. She would later learn that the reason for the discount was that the owner of the franchise was one of Jackson Hand's *"flies in the web."*

When she was walking out to her car, she saw Jay West parking his pick-up in the lot. He got out and said, "You a new Hand?"

"Brand new," she said with a warm smile. Jay noticed that her eyes were so dark that they seemed to reflect very fine points of light even from an overcast sky. He found himself helplessly staring at them.

"Have you known Mr. Hand very long?"

"I just met him. He seems okay."

"You might want to re-think your decision to work here," he said.

"What makes you say that?" she asked. "I don't think I'll have to have a lot of contact with him if I don't want to. I'll just do my job and collect my check."

She could see that Jay was clearly uncomfortable talking to her. She wondered what his problem was. He walked over closer to where she was standing and said, "You seem like a really nice girl. I'll bet you could make a killing as a waitress with your looks."

"I couldn't make this kind of money even at three-quarter's pay."

"There, you see what I mean? What kind of excuse did he give you for only offering three-quarter's pay?"

Nellie wasn't comfortable disclosing the particular conditions of her employment with someone she had just met. She knew she was innocent, but she had been to prison, and Jay West was no more likely to believe her side of the story than Mr. Hand had been.

"It's just until I complete my training," she lied. She wasn't about to allude to her trial period.

"Well, good luck. My name's Jay West. I hope I see you around," he said.

"Nice to meet you, Jay. I'm Nellie Brighton."

"Pretty name for a pretty lady," said West.

"Why thank you, Mr. West," she said in her best Blanche Dubois accent.

"See ya'," he said disappearing into the building.

Maybe he was a nice guy after all. What a nice thing to say, *"Pretty name for a pretty lady."* Still, she wondered why he acted so strangely. *Oh well, he's probably harmless enough.*

Chapter Two

The next day Nellie arrived at the Jacks and Hands office dressed in her new Reebok Cross Trainers and a new white T-shirt and jeans. The first thing that the training coordinator said was, "My name is Cathy Garvey, and I'm going to get you started. Come over here and sit on the table. I have to get a blood sample."

"A blood sample? What for?" asked Nellie.

"Drug testing, and we also test you for infectious diseases. You know, Hepatitis B, AIDS, that type of thing. It's really for your own good. Wouldn't you want to know if you had a disease?"

"Sure, I guess so. It's just that I didn't know about it, that's all."

"Didn't Mr. Hand go over the rules with you?"

"Yes, but I thought all I had to do was pee in a cup," she said.

"You can pee all you want, but I need a blood sample," said Garvey.

Nellie gave the training coordinator a sample of her blood and her measurements for a uniform. Garvey then asked her, "What's your bra size?"

15

"My bra size?" she asked. "I don't see what that has to do with anything."

"It does if you want one to fit," said Garvey. "You are required to wear company issued sets of underwear. It's all part of putting up the right impression for our customers. You've seen sheer underwear that reveals the shape of the breast. Some of them are very thin. Mr. Hand won't allow that kind of thing on any of the Hands. We take care of families, Ms. Brighton. Just think of yourself as Mary Poppins for a while."

"Okay, but I don't have much of a singing voice," she said jokingly.

"You probably won't be called upon to sing," said Garvey clearly not getting the joke. "So, what is your bra size?" asked Garvey again.

"Thirty-four B," said Nellie.

"And your panties?" asked Garvey.

"Who's gonna' see my panties?" asked Nellie. "Is all this really necessary?"

"Try to act professionally, Ms. Brighton. I'm sure that all the reasons for our company rules will become clear to you in time."

"I'm a size four panty. My height is five foot eight, my weight is one eighteen, and my measurements are thirty-four - twenty-five - thirty-six. Is that enough information for you?"

"Now I can issue you the proper uniform. You will receive four shirts, three pairs of pants and five pairs of socks along with five sets of underwear. If you need replacements in the future, they can be purchased from the company and the charges will be automatically deducted from your paycheck. Place your clothes in a locker; the combination is on the inside of the door. Please make a note of it. You will get dressed into a Hand uniform and report with me to your cooking class."

"Yes, Mrs. Garvey," said Nellie. She felt like she had just joined the army.

Chapter Three

The next week seemed to fly by as Nellie learned the finer points of gourmet cooking, shopping and preparing meals that were registered with the Jacks and Hands inventory. If a family requested Veal Francais with white asparagus spears, freshly baked French sourdough and a Caesar salad for nine people, Nellie was expected to know where to shop for the finest ingredients and to be able to prepare and present the meal at a precise time of day. A typical meal-prep took roughly three hours from start to finish, and since the customer was billed for a minimum of four, the fourth hour was a bonus. Cooking was much more preferable to cleaning because the customer always utilized the four-hour purchase of maid service. After a day of cleaning a large home, Nellie's back would often bother her until she could settle down into a warm tub or a hot shower. The company had an in-house chiropractor that could be used by the staff for brief intervals on their time off. There was also a staff physician who could issue prescriptions and perform various types of outpatient procedures on the Jacks and Hands. This was far more cost efficient than paying health insurance premiums for a staff of twenty-four people.

It was explained to Nellie that it was in the company's best interest to keep a healthy staff to head off any potential liability suit from their customers. With the recent threat of biological terrorism many people were reluctant to place their trust in strangers. That was the basic appeal of Jacks and Hands. A customer didn't really care who pulled the weeds or cut the lawn, but who would actually be occupying their kitchen and tutoring their children was another matter entirely. Soon Nellie was beginning to be requested by a number of families. She thought that she was not only making money in order to return to college, but that she was also making friends. One day she was called into the clinic where she was informed that she may have been exposed to a minor strain of viral meningitis. She was assured that there was nothing to worry about as long as she took a booster of antibiotics provided by the staff physician. He gave her two pills that were to be taken four hours apart, handing her the first one with a glass of water. She obediently swallowed the pill. Then she put the second pill in her pocket and went to her next assignment.

She was faux painting a living room for a woman named Joyce Everly. She used a rag-rolling technique taught to her by the painting instructors at Jacks and Hands. Mrs. Everly left for a few hours to keep a hair appointment and a luncheon date. While she was gone, her husband came home and found Nellie hard at work on the living-room walls.

"Very clever," said the man. She had already applied the base coat of paint and was blending the complimentary color while it was still wet.

"Hi, Mr. Everly, I'm Nellie. Forgive me for not getting down and shaking your hand, but I have to apply this second color while the walls are still workable."

"Oh, that's okay, Nellie," he said with a smile. "No need to apologize. You'll just have to make it up to me later," he admired her shape as she stood on a ladder.

"Sure thing," she said trying to be friendly.

Having finished applying the living room base coat, she went to the kitchen to wash the water-based paint off of her hands. While she was standing at the sink, Mr. Everly brushed his hips against her backside briefly as he was getting a beer glass out of an upper cabinet.

"Excuse me, Nellie," he said.

"No problem, Mr. Everly. How do you like the living-room?" she asked.

"I think it looks very nice. I think that *you* look very nice, too, Nellie. Has anyone ever told you that lately?" he asked.

Thinking of Jay West in the parking lot of Jacks and Hands, she said, "As a matter of fact, yes."

"I'm not surprised," said Bill Everly. "Not a bit surprised at all."

"Can I trouble you for a glass of water, Mr. Everly?" she asked. "I have to take a pill."

"Certainly, Dear. Help yourself. There's ice in the dispenser on the door of the fridge. The glasses are right above you."

"Thanks," she said. "Tell Mrs. Everly to let me know if she decides to go ahead with your daughter Cindy's room. You can tell her I can do it in about four hours."

"Will do. I'll see if I can talk her into it," said Everly.

"Thanks," said Nellie. "Gotta' go."

Chapter Four

The next day Nellie woke up with a serious headache. She supposed that she had inhaled too many paint fumes and it was affecting her somehow. The last thing she remembered was soaking in a tub after she had gotten home from the Everly's. She was dressed in panties and a nightshirt, but she didn't even remember *going* to bed. She didn't feel particularly hungry, but she didn't really remember having dinner as well. *That's strange. Those paint fumes are stronger than I thought.* She showered and ate a light breakfast before setting off to work. When she reached the Jacks and Hands building, Jay West was just coming out of the door. She raised her head and was about to speak to him when he held up his hand as if to say, *not now Nellie.*

"Jay, what's wrong?" she asked as he walked silently by her.

"God damn it, Nellie. Now he's got his hooks in you. Don't say I didn't warn you," said West.

She watched him walk to his truck, get inside, and slam the door shut. She saw him shaking his head as he drove away. *Now* what's going on? *Why can't anyone be normal,* she wondered. She went into the office to pick up

22

her assignment for the day from Susan Cole, the woman who scheduled them. Cathy Garvey gave her a dark look and said, "Mr. Hand would like a word with you, Ms. Brighton."

"Mr. Hand?" she asked. "What does he want?"

"You'll have to ask him that yourself," said Garvey.

Nellie walked up to Hand's office and knocked on the door.

"Come in," she heard from inside the office. She opened the door and asked, "Mr. Hand, you wanted to see me?" She felt a definite tightness in her stomach muscles.

"Yes. Close the door and have a seat," said Hand. "We have something to discuss."

"Oh?" she asked feeling the severity of the moment. She sat down in a chair.

"Yes," he said. "We have to discuss whether or not you're going back to prison to complete your sentence. It's two years if I'm not mistaken."

"What are you talking about?" she couldn't stop her hands from shaking.

"I'd like you to look at these pictures, Ms. Brighton. Tell me what you see?"

Nellie took a large envelope from his outstretched hand. She slipped out a large stack of photographs and placed them in her lap. She recognized herself immediately. She was appalled to see that she was naked. She was sitting on the couch in her apartment without a stitch of clothes on.

Her eyes were sleepy and her head was hanging to the side toward the naked body of Jay West. There was a crack pipe in her hand and a number of pills spilled on the coffee table in front of her.

"Tell me what you see, Ms. Brighton," said Hand.

"I see a set up," said Nellie. "I see a sick bastard's attempt to frame me like I was framed once before."

"A very successful attempt I might add. The evidence is very damning."

"So, you've got a bunch of naked pictures of me. So what? That's not a crime as far as I know."

"Perhaps not. However, your parole officer might be interested to learn that the glassine bag pictured in front of your naked body has your fingerprints all over it, as does the crack pipe as well."

"Okay, I know when I'm licked," said Nellie. "What's it gonna' cost me this time?" she asked. A large tear escaped from her eye and fell on the naked body of Jay West in the photograph.

"Not very much at all," said Hand. "Just your cooperation in a little matter involving William Everly. Mr. Everly is in a very powerful position to block my acquisition of an oceanfront property necessary to complete a hotel complex and strip mall that has been four years in the development stage. But that doesn't concern you, Ms.

Brighton. All you need to know is that I need to obtain a videotape of you engaged in sex with him."

Nellie began to cry.

"There, there, now, Ms. Brighton. You'll be pleased to know that after this little favor, you will be given all the photographs of yourself and Mr. West, as well as the crack pipe and the glassine baggy. Doesn't that sound fair?"

"There's nothing fair about it," said Nellie.

"Well, I'm also willing to give you full pay for the remainder of your assignments. Do we have a deal?"

"What choice do I have?"

"None," said Hand. "Now, what can you tell me about a possible site for video surveillance?"

"There's an A/C vent in his study that'll work," she said.

"Excellent. A Jack is scheduled to oil the wood paneling later this week. Let me ask you, Nellie, was he . . . interested?"

"You mean Everly? Yeah, he was interested."

"From the looks of the photographs, I can't say as I blame him. You have a very nice body, Nellie."

"Go fuck yourself, Hand. I'll do this one job for you, but if you screw me, I promise that somehow I'll kill you."

"Relax, Nellie. A deal's a deal. You'll find that there is a certain honor among thieves."

"Yeah, I'll bet," said Nellie facetiously.

"Seriously, Nellie. I don't want to control your life. I just need your body for one job only. I stand to make thousands from Mr. Everly before ever forcing him to relinquish control over the sale of the property I want. In fact, he'll practically buy it for me. I happen to know that he doesn't have a pre-nuptial agreement with his wife - his lawyer is one of our rather committed clients if you know what I mean. If she sued for divorce, she would take half of his considerable fortune in this community property state of ours. He's actually getting off pretty cheap."

"I don't think anybody gets off cheap around you," said Nellie.

"Think about it, Nellie. If Everly could keep it in his pants, he would have nothing to worry about. It's a victimless crime. You have to be a creep in the first place to put   yourself in a vulnerable situation. Wouldn't you agree?" he asked.

"I don't think he would act on his fantasies if he wasn't tempted in his own house. That's what makes it wrong. He's a victim all right. So, when do I have to do the dirty deed?" she asked.

"I'll let you know. We'll put off any requests for a Hand until the camera is in place," said Hand.

"Can I ask you something?" said Nellie.

"Fire away," said Hand.

"What is it that you have on Jay West?"

"Ahh, Mr. West," teased Hand. "Your fellow crack orgy partner," he said chuckling.

"What was his crime that you're feeding on?" she demanded.

"That's the beauty of the situation. He has committed no crime, yet!"

"What do you mean, yet?" she asked.

"About a month ago a sixteen-year-old lovely was brutally raped inside a theme park here in central Florida. The rapist stuffed a sock in her mouth so she couldn't scream. Although the area was dark, she managed to see her assailant rather clearly. He had blond hair and a blond mustache. Sound like anyone you know?" he asked snickering.

"Jay doesn't seem like the rapist type to me," she said.

"Indeed, he isn't. The girl's description would never be enough to convict him, but unfortunately his semen was found on the girl's underpants. The girl probably didn't notice that the rapist used a condom so the obvious assumption is to match the DNA to the semen and you have your rapist. A simple phone call could solve this crime for them. Do you think it's time for me to do my civic duty, Nellie?"

"When does he get his freedom?" she asked.

"Soon. Very soon. He's just about outlived his usefulness."

"What's that supposed to mean? You're going to kill him?"

"Nothing so sinister, I assure you. He'll soon be free to leave as long as he signs a confidentiality agreement. Actually, his last useful assignment was that touching little encounter with you."

"Did he rape me?" asked Nellie.

"I honestly don't know. I wasn't there. All I was concerned with was obtaining the photographs and the fingerprint evidence."

"I thought you might get your jollies by taking the pictures yourself," she said.

"I'm afraid I don't much care for comatose women, Nellie. But now that you've regained your consciousness, take off your clothes."

"What?"

"I said take off your clothes, Nellie. You heard me."

"What if I don't?" she asked.

"I don't care if you go back to prison or not. I can always use another girl to get to Everly. Do you take off your clothes or do I make the call?"

Nellie started to cry. She pulled her shirt over her head revealing the bra that the company required that she wear. She kicked off her shoes and undid the clasp on the bra behind her back. The bra fell away revealing her breasts. She then undid her pants and slid them to the floor. She pulled off her panties and was standing in front of Hand wearing only her socks.

"Keep going," he said.

Still crying she removed her socks and stood naked before him. He walked over to her and grasped her right nipple between his middle and index finger. Her chest heaved slightly as her stifled crying continued. She didn't want to give the bastard the satisfaction of knowing how much he was hurting her pride. She was completely degraded standing before him, forced to obey his every command. He said to her, "Just so we have an understanding here, Nellie. Let's not forget who has the upper hand. Now get dressed and get out."

Chapter Five

Nellie left the office of Jacks and Hands and went straight to the beach. She didn't bother stopping at the desk to get an assignment for the day. After all, she didn't need to worry about being fired. Hand had her in place for an assignment that would compromise a very powerful man. She was still a valuable pawn in his end game. What she didn't count on was that Jay West had also blown off his assignment for the day and had followed her. She walked along the shore with her chest quaking from time to time, feeling that she had never felt so miserable in all her life. When the drug dealer in the nightclub set her up, at least she was just a patsy. She knew the girl had nothing against her. It was merely survival of the fittest. But Hand didn't need her to protect himself. He was a force of evil as treacherous as any serpent in the Bible, possibly even worse. Lucifer, though treacherous, was a fallen Angel who dared to compare himself to the Creator. Hand was evil for evil's sake. He was a man born without a conscience.

After a while she turned around and saw Jay West walking a hundred feet behind her. She instantly turned around again and began to run. She wanted to put as much distance between them that was humanly possible in the shortest amount of time. He called to her, "Nellie, wait!" She kept on running. He continued on after her, "For God's sake, would you just wait?" was his pleading cry.

Oh sure, God! Why don't we bring God into it? Whatever's going on here God has nothing to do with it. Perhaps that's the problem. God is indifferent. She did nothing but go to college to try to be a better writer. She did nothing but offer to help a friend find her way around at school. She did nothing but try to do a good job and earn an honest wage. And yet she found herself standing naked in front of a very evil man earlier in the day ready to perform whatever obscene act he wished against her will. Her freedom was gone. She didn't have her life anymore. And there was no promise that she could ever regain it by her own hand. She was reduced to the mercy of her tormentor as was the asshole chasing after her. She turned around briefly and said, "Go away, you asshole! I think you've done enough!" She ran for all she was worth. There was a spirit rising up inside of her. She wouldn't be defeated now. Not after all of her ugly little acts of degradation. There was nothing left to lose. She felt she could run faster than her body would let her and burst her heart. Who would care anyway? Her life was over.

She suddenly felt hands grasping her waist as she fell violently to the ground as she tried to fend them off.

"Jesus, Nellie. I've never seen a woman run so fast."

"Get the fuck away from me, you rapist!" she said through panting and tears.

"Rapist?" protested West. "I've never raped a woman in my life."

"Oh, so I was a willing partner just because I was passed out?" she asked.

"Is that what you think?" his voice began to rise. "Is that the kind of person you think I am?" he said fuming.

"I don't give a fuck. Just leave me alone," she said.

"I'm a victim, too," he reasoned. "What would you have done in my. . ."

"Just. . . leave me the fuck alone, West. Do I have to spell it out for you any better than that? I can make the phone call to the Orlando Police Department as easily as Hand can."

"You think I raped that girl, then," he challenged.

"No, I don't. But I saw some pictures of you sitting naked with me on my sofa. What am I supposed to think about that?"

"Nothing happened, I swear. It's not that I don't find you attractive, but I would never take advantage of a girl in a situation like that. I believe that sex is something to be mutually agreed upon," he said. "Do you think I would have had my way with you while you were unconscious?"

"I don't know you. I have no idea what you're capable of."

"Okay, that's fair enough," he said getting up off of the sand and brushing himself off. "But let me tell you one thing you don't know. I was given a choice. I could produce the pictures with you once you passed out, or I could let them go ahead with three other Jacks to do the job, and you can take my word for it, they would have raped you." He started to walk away when Nellie said, "Are you telling me the truth?"

"No, I'm a lying rapist, Nellie, but you're safe for now, aren't you? I'm walking the other way."

"Jay, wait!" she said. "I'm so confused. How do we get out of this trap we're in?"

"I'm not exactly sure. But I know one thing. I could use a friend, Nellie," said West. "I swear I never touched you. I knew it wouldn't be right. I thought that maybe we could have a chance together to get away from Jacks and Hands."

"I think I'm all out of chances, Jay. I'm damaged goods."

"Me, too," said West. "So, what now? What's the bastard want you to do?"

"Hand wants me to get Bill Everly into bed, so he can blackmail him."

"I'm sorry, Nellie. I realize that he's got you between a rock and a hard place."

"Tell me about it."

"If it means anything to you, I just want you to know that I don't think any less of you for doing his bidding."

"Well, whoop-de-do," said Nellie. "An unwilling prostitute forgives an unwilling prostitute. What a happy ending that can promise."

"Well, couldn't it?" he protested. "I didn't ask to be a pawn either. What's wrong with me that isn't wrong with you? We all have to pick up our lives somehow, Nellie. I'd like to be there when it's time to pick up yours."

"One thing at a time," she said. "Suppose that you've picked up something that you didn't want from one of your customers?"

"I've only had one sexual encounter with a customer. She gave me oral sex. I don't think I could pick up anything nasty from that."

"Well, did you enjoy it?" asked Nellie.

"Not really. The only way I could finish was thinking about someone like you. When she was finished, she just about ran out of the room. Hand told me later what she did."

"Hand told me he collected your seed to frame you."

"You got it," he said. "The woman was compromised before she ever had contact with me. Her only way out was to deliver my seed to Hand. Believe me, no one has gotten it since."

"Well, that's something," said Nellie. "Who was she?" she asked.

"As a matter of fact, it was Joyce Everly," said West.

Nellie started laughing.

"What?" asked West. "What is it?"

"It might be our ticket out of this mess," said Nellie.

"What do you mean?" asked West.

"Well, I'm supposed to seduce Everly, right?"

"Yeah, so?"

"You seduced Mrs. Everly, right?"

"Well, actually it was her idea."

"So, suppose I tip off Mr. Everly about what's going on, but get him to go through with it?"

"You're going to invite him to have sex with you on camera? What will that prove?"

"Don't be so crude. We can appear to be doing it without actually *doing it*."

"I still don't get it. What's to be gained by playing Hand's game?"

"He'll have film that's no good to him. Everly will tip off his wife before she ever sees the tape if it ever comes to that with the understanding that he's trying to sting Hand for blackmail. We're both willing partners, and even if the tape of Mrs. Everly ever surfaces, we can probably get it suppressed. After all it's not a crime to do an adult film. But blackmail is an entirely different matter. I think that the

Everly marriage will survive it, and as soon as I get the damning evidence against me, we're home free."

"But I'm still vulnerable," said West. "All it takes is a phone call and I'm toast."

"Maybe not. He had to have another Jack assault the girl. Maybe she can identify him instead of you. Mrs. Everly will testify that she delivered your seed to Hand. Maybe they can identify her saliva on the girl's panties as well."

"It's not there. I pulled out at the last second. I think she got it off her chest," said West. "In either case, I'll stand by you if you'll stand by me. I'm willing to give us a chance, Nellie."

"I think it could be a good end to a bad beginning," said Nellie. "I'm looking forward to the chance to know you away from all of Hand's evil."

"We'll be very lucky to get through this, Nellie. Tomorrow we have to go back to work like nothing ever happened."

"Okay, I can do that. Besides, I need the money. Hand promised me full pay now that he has me in his web. I'm going to take advantage of it while I can."

"He won't be able to use you for very long, Nellie. Now you've got friends on your side."

Chapter Six

The next day Joyce Everly was forced into the uncomfortable position of having to hire a Jack. A Jack was the last thing Mrs. Everly wanted to think about let alone invite into her home after her ordeal orchestrated by Hand. Her husband had asked her to hire a Jack to oil the expensive wood paneling in his study. They had been putting it off for too long and the wood was in danger of drying out and cracking from the harsh Florida sunlight. Her husband would know if she hired someone other than a Jack and would want to know why. The Jack truck outside your property was thought to be a symbol of prestige for some people, and Bill Everly was one of those people. He was a prominent real estate developer who recommended Jacks and Hands to all of his wealthy customers. The Jacks and Hands popularity was enjoying a kind of *"snob appeal."*

She couldn't find a way out of her dilemma, so she made the call.

"Jacks and Hands," answered the friendly voice of Susan Cole the receptionist.

"This is Joyce Everly, Susan."

"Hi, Mrs. Everly. What can I do for you?" asked Susan.

"I need a Jack as soon as possible. Bill wants his study walls treated."

"Do we have it on file?" she asked referring to the procedure being a standing order performed on a regular-basis.

"I think so. We usually have it done once a year."

"Can you hold, please?"

"Sure." Joyce Everly listened to the annoying jingle, *Jacks and Hands* while she waited briefly on hold. Susan returned after about fifteen seconds, "Are you there?"

"I'm here," said Joyce in a tired voice.

"It is a standing order. We treat his study with Thompson's Tung Oil. It requires one Jack for one block of time. That's two hundred forty dollars plus materials," she said.

"Whatever. When can I expect him, Susan?"

"I'll have someone out there by noon."

"Thanks, Susan."

"You're welcome. Helping hands are just a call away," said Susan before she hung up. She was required to recite the last line of the jingle to close a phone conversation. It never failed to rub Joyce Everly the wrong way since her ordeal. After she replaced the receiver, she said quietly, "Fuck you very much, Susan." She supposed she was being

38

unfair, but she didn't care. Susan Cole had no idea that she was working for a monster. Neither did Cathy Garvey or a dozen other people on the Jacks and Hands payroll. There were only twelve current sexual operatives, or *stable members,* out of twenty-four Jacks and Hands. Five were Jacks and seven were Hands. Nellie was the most recent addition to their number. Jay had been a Jack for eighteen months, but only recently became part of the stable with the job he did on Nellie. As luck would have it, Jay was next up on the rotation and was called upon to do the work on the walls of Everly's study.

Jackson Hand made sure that one of the five Jacks of the stable would respond to the Everlys. He needed the remote-controlled video device installed in the study's air conditioning vent. Joyce Everly met Jay at the door, "Before you say a word, let me tell you what that bastard did to me."

"It must have been something to make you be a willing part of a conspiracy to rape a young girl and frame me for it," he fumed.

"I knew nothing about the rape," she protested.

"Well, what the hell did you *think* he was going to do with my semen?"

"He told me he was going to freeze it and *threaten* to frame you, that's all."

"Well, that's enough," said West.

"I swear I knew nothing about the plans to hurt that poor girl. I would have let him ruin me rather than stand by for that."

"So, what did he do to you? Was it video?"

"Yes, but not like it was with you."

"You weren't giving someone oral sex? Is that what you mean?"

"You and I were just going through the motions, you know that. You had no feelings for me, and I didn't have any for you. We were just having sex, right?"

"Yeah, so?" asked West.

"Well, I fell in love with someone. He caught me on video making love. *Real passion.* You can easily tell the difference," she said with tears in her eyes.

"You seemed to be enjoying yourself with me," he said angrily, "until you gathered my seed into a film canister, you *Bitch!*"

"Oh, don't act so innocent with *me,* you little shit. What did he have on you?" she demanded.

"Nothing."

"Nothing? Why did you let yourself get seduced?"

"I don't know. Why does anyone let himself get seduced? Hand said you were a good customer and to treat you like a queen."

"Oh well that makes it fine and dandy, doesn't it? All you did was try to make a little money for getting a blow job," she said through angry tears.

"I'm sorry. I know I was wrong," he said, "but so were you. I like the sound of prostitute a hell of a lot better than extortionist or conspirator."

"We make a fine pair. You thought you were taking advantage of a lonely older woman when actually I was taking advantage of you."

"So, tell me why you did it?" he asked.

"I told you. I was caught on tape with my lover," she said through new tears.

"So why didn't you leave your husband? He's got plenty of money."

"The scandal would have ruined him. And my twelve-year-old daughter."

"Oh, come on. People survive that kind of controversy every day," said West.

"No, they don't, Jay. My lover is a woman, and not one of the Hands. She has nothing to do with that bastard's company. He just got lucky. He was trying to catch Bill and me in an uncompromising situation when he got me on tape with my female lover. She's married, too, and it would have destroyed both of us. She has *two* young daughters."

"Jesus," he said.

"So, there you have it."

"There might be a way out of this. For both of us," said West.

"Really?" she asked daring to have hope in her eyes.

"There's a Hand who got framed also who's got an idea that just might work."

"I'm listening," she said wiping her eyes with her palms.

"We have to involve your husband, Bill."

"Forget it."

"Wait a minute. Just hear me out, okay?"

"Go ahead," she said wearily.

"Suppose the Hand gets your husband to come on to her and we get it on tape?"

"Yeah, and?"

"Let's say they stop before anything happens, but they've got their clothes off."

"Keep going," she said.

"Well getting that on tape kind of gets you off the hook in case he ever learns of your infidelity, but I don't think he ever has to know about it if we pull it off."

"I'm not following you, Jay."

"Just listen. After we get him on tape, the Hand comes back to your husband and tells him that she has him on tape."

"So, she's blackmailing him?"

"Not really. She tells him that Mr. Hand has her between a rock and a hard place and enlists his help. She asks him to make a fake sex tape to trap Jackson Hand in his blackmailing operation. If he refuses, then she threatens him with the real tape. You and I will be here during the taping so your husband knows that you're not going to get any surprises by Hand. Understand?"

"So how does that trap him?" she asked.

"When your husband gets the tape, he goes to the police and charges Hand with blackmail and extortion. They arrest Hand and impound all the dirty evidence he has on everyone. He keeps it all in a safe in his office. It'll never become public and a lot of people will be off the hook. The evidence will be inadmissible in all the cases except the one against Hand. Bingo. He's out of business."

"But what about you, Jay? Your semen is on that girl's underpants."

"I think I've got that covered, too. Can we count on your help?"

"I think that all of this has to start with Bill. He has to take the bait."

"Believe me, he will," said West.

"Who's the girl? The Hand?" she asked.

"Nellie Brighton."

"She's lovely," said Joyce Everly.

"Yeah, your husband thinks so, too."

43

Chapter Seven

Nellie received an assignment to cater a small dinner party the next day. She was to serve a beef tenderloin with twice-baked potatoes, creamed onions, French cut green beans with slithered almonds, and key lime pie for dessert. The hosts would choose their own wine from their wine cellar. She was running a little late having just come from the butcher and still needing to pick up the fresh produce when her cell phone rang, "Hello," she said.

"Nellie, it's Jay. How you doin'?"

"I'm late," she said. "I'm cooking for eight people who want to sit down in two-and-a-half hours. I'm still about forty minutes away from getting there so it's gonna' be close. What's up?" she asked wondering why he called.

"It's all set up. Joyce Everly's gonna' work with us."

"Sure, why wouldn't she? She has a lot less to lose than you do if it doesn't work."

"Don't be so sure, Nellie."

"What's that supposed to mean?" she asked.

"It wasn't just a sex sting; it was a love sting."

"Huh?" asked Nellie clearly not understanding.

"I'll tell you about it later. Who you cooking for?" asked West.

"Lucy Brooks, her husband, her daughters and another family of four."

"I get the picture," said West. "I'll let you go."

"Thanks. Call me around seven."

"Okay, bye."

"Bye," said Nellie just arriving at the fresh produce stand.

Nellie's dinner-prep went well, and the Brooks family seemed very grateful for her help. They were able to entertain their guests without having to worry about a thing. When she presented the meal on their fine china and sterling silver flatware, the table looked beautiful. She told them to load the dishes in the dishwasher but not to bother running it. She would return in the morning to do them by hand. It was all part of the package. When the Brooks family and their guests were seated at the table, Nellie excused herself and drove to her home. At seven o'clock sharp, she got a call from Jay West.

"How'd your dinner party go?" he asked

"Fine, it was easy. They had me cook beef tenderloin and all you have to do is bake it for forty minutes at four hundred degrees. Piece of cake. The only hard thing was making the pie crust, but I'm getting pretty good at it."

"Joyce Everly is going to ask for you to do Cindy's room tomorrow. Her husband has been coming home for lunch lately. She's going to conveniently forget something and have to run out to the store. She'll be gone for about twenty-five minutes so you have to time it right. She'll come back after about fifteen unexpectedly, so it'll be a race to get your clothes back on."

"If she's late, I swear I'm gonna' tell him I have herpes or something," she said.

West started laughing, "I don't think it'll come to that, but it's not a bad idea. On second thought better make it AIDS."

"What if he has a condom?" she asked seriously.

"You're right-stick to genital herpes. Tell him he can still get it with a condom," suggested West.

"The poor sap. He's just getting set up like everyone else," she said.

"It's for a good cause, Nellie. Hopefully, it'll even get his wife off the hook."

"I hope so. How are you going to get the bug into Hand's office?" asked Nellie knowing she could get Hand to implicate the real rapist and thereby get West off the hook.

"I might need your help with that one," he said. "I've got to get past Susan Cole."

"We'll put a ding in her car. That should do it," said Nellie.

"You're pretty devious, Brighton. Remind me to stay on your good side."

"You better," she said laughing. She hadn't laughed in a while and it felt particularly good. She finally admitted to herself that Jay West made her feel good.

"Did you eat yet?" asked West.

"No, and I'm starving. I was thinking of ordering a pizza."

"Would you let me bring one over?" he suggested hopefully.

"I guess that would be okay," she said casually.

"Great!" he said. "I know a really good place. I'll also pick up a nice dry red wine."

"Aren't you afraid I might take advantage of you?" she asked slyly.

His silence for a full ten seconds made her almost sorry that her dig hit the target.

"Yeah, well it'll probably take me about a half-hour," he said. "Can you hold on for that long?"

"I'll try, but I might start eating the furniture."

"I'm on my way."

She examined her feelings while West was getting the wine and the pizza. She found him attractive enough. That's why Hand made him a member of his stable. He seemed to have a heart also, which was remarkable considering the obvious torment he was going through. It appeared as though he were struggling to emerge from a dark shadowy world that was sure to overcome him the minute his guard was down. She couldn't stand in his shoes, so she was reluctant to judge him. After all, what if he had begged-out of the frame-up that Hand had orchestrated to trap her. She might have been raped repeatedly and Hand would never even know or care. In a way West had become the best of all evils for her. He protected her even as he set up the camera and placed the crack pipe in her hands. At least he had some feelings for her and would never abuse her while she was unconscious. That counted for something, didn't it? She found herself waiting anxiously for his arrival. When she was changing clothes, she noticed that her shirt reeked of a long day of work. She decided that she had time to shower and put on just the slightest hint of musk scented cologne. A University of Central Florida T-shirt felt a lot better than her Hands logo uniform and she was feeling relaxed for the first time all day. The telephone rang, and she went to the living room to take the call there. The voice on the phone said, "Ms. Brighton?"

"That's right. Who's this?" she asked wanting to cut to the chase. If he had to ask that meant he wasn't sure, and if he wasn't sure that spelled *salesman.*

"My name is Sidney Campbell. You might remember me from your trial?" he asked.

"You were the prosecutor, right?"

"That's right," he said.

"Well, you did a fine job, didn't you?"

"That's what I'm calling about, Ms. Brighton. Perhaps I didn't."

"What the hell are you talking about?" she said shaking.

"Relax, Ms. Brighton. I'm calling as a friend."

"Uh huh, what for?" she asked suspiciously.

"I have reason to believe that you received a less than adequate defense."

"So, what do you care? You're with the District Attorney's office, right?"

"We're not all bad, Ms. Brighton, and now I work in the private sector."

"So, what's that got to do with me? I paid my debt to society," said Nellie issuing a silent prayer that Hand had not turned over the evidence against her.

"That's the whole point, Nellie. Maybe you never needed to. May I call you Nellie?" asked Campbell.

"Knock yourself out," she said dryly.

Campbell chuckled briefly and said, "There's been an interesting turn of events that I feel I have no choice but to bring to your attention."

"Which is?"

"I've recently learned that you have been deceived by your defense attorney."

It took a little while for the information to sink in. Finally, she asked, "So what can I do about it?"

"Well, I can't guarantee anything, but I'd venture a guess that you could be awarded a sizable malpractice settlement."

"By sizeable you mean what? A thousand bucks or something?"

"I'd say more like a million. Give or take a hundred thousand."

Nellie was in shock. She sat with the phone to her ear in silence until the lawyer said, "Nellie?"

"I'm still here," she said dully.

"Did you hear what I said," asked Campbell.

"I thought all you guys stuck together. You know, like doctors," she suggested.

"Yeah, we stick together when we're only doing our jobs, and somebody complains, but in this case, someone didn't do his job. In fact, he went out of his way *not* to do his job. That's the reason for this phone call."

"I still don't understand, Mr. Campbell," said Nellie.

"Do you remember the girl, Sheila Bradley?" he asked.

"My brother's girlfriend's friend, do I ever. That's when all my troubles started."

"Well, she may have done you a huge favor," said Campbell.

"By sending me to prison?" asked Nellie.

"In a way, yes."

"This has got to be good. Okay, tell me what's going on," she demanded.

"About seven months ago Ms. Bradley was arrested for possession of a controlled substance."

"Drugs," said Nellie.

"Drugs," confirmed Campbell. "Anyway, from her jail cell she decided to own up to all the nasty deeds she had done to get her into her present position. One of the things she mentioned was putting the Ecstasy tablets in your purse just prior to the police raid."

"Too little too late, right?"

"No, not right. That's the whole point. You hadn't gone to trial yet, and she claims to have told your defense attorney the whole story."

"So how can that help me now? I can't prove it, can I?"

"As a matter of fact, you can. At least I think you can," said Campbell.

"How?"

"Well, let me start from the beginning. When Mr. Sorrell was defending you, he fended off the public defender, Ms. Eva Grange. He told Ms. Grange that she didn't have a chance in hell at getting your charges reduced or dropped and that she should turn over all her notes to him if she cared anything about your welfare. Subsequently, she did.

Mr. Sorrell got your case and pleaded guilty to possession but not with intent to sell. That defense was doomed from the start because all the drugs were individually wrapped. A person doesn't carry around a month's supply of recreational drugs. Well, here's the real kicker. Sheila Bradley confessed to putting the drugs in your purse and the deposition was filed with the original Defense Attorney's office, which happened to be Eva Grange. Mr. Sorrell's office declined to attend the "discovery" session of your trial. During discovery, all the facts in your favor would have caught up to you. Eva Grange's office forwarded the deposition to Mr. Sorrell's office and he neglected to include it. But it gets even better than that. Sorrell had to sign for a return receipt letter from Grange's office. That proves that he received the deposition from the Bradley woman and decided not to introduce it. I should have known that something was up when he abstained from the discovery session. In all honesty, I was only interested in chalking up another conviction and considered that one to be a freebie. We're not perfect, Nellie. The system isn't perfect. But perhaps the wrong that was done to you can be righted. Mr. Sorrell has represented many powerful drug dealers in the past and has amassed a considerable fortune. Can you think of any reason that he might have for wanting you to go to prison?"

"Oh yeah," she said. "He delivered me to another slime-ball who used and abused me."

JACKS & HANDS

"I can't represent you in the case against Mr. Sorrell because I was working for the District Attorney's office at the time. However, I can turn your case over to a very competent woman who I'm sure will produce the results in your best interest. You're about to become a very rich woman, Nellie."

"I've got a question for you, Mr. Campbell." she said.

"I'll be glad to help if I can," he said.

"A friend of mine was framed or almost framed for a rape he didn't commit."

"You're sure he's innocent?" asked Campbell.

"Absolutely. Well, here's the deal. We think we can get another man to admit who the rapist actually was. If we can get him on tape is that admissible evidence in court?"

"Well, a taped conversation is admissible if one of the persons gives their consent."

"That's it?"

"Basically, yes. That's it."

"Cool," said Nellie. "Thank you, Mr. Campbell. You've just made my day."

"You're welcome, Nellie. Someone from my firm will definitely be in touch."

"Thanks, Mr. Campbell," said Nellie.

"You're welcome. And call me Sidney. I'm sure we'll meet again."

"Thanks, Sidney."

"Again, you're welcome," he said and then broke the connection.

Chapter Eight

When Nellie Brighton woke up the next day, the world looked suddenly brighter. She had been dealt a bad hand of cards during the last six months, but her luck was about to change. She didn't dare to hope for what the lawyer, Mr. Campbell, had said was possible. But she had new hope that her plan with Jay West could bring about a positive change for a lot of people. Whether or not they were innocent of all the charges that Hand held against them, she knew that he was exploiting them horribly. Unless you go through the nightmare of exploitation, you don't really understand the totality of its hopeless circumstance. All of the people that Hand had trapped were dreaming of the day when they could even the odds. It was all that they lived for in some cases. Nellie couldn't believe that Hand could be so arrogant that he would gamble his whole future on a house of cards. She couldn't wait to be the one person to pull out the critical card. Jay West felt the same way. On the one hand he was afraid that Jackson Hand might be able to implicate him in a rape he never committed, and on the other hand, he felt he couldn't let the operation go on any longer and create more of the kind of pain he was experiencing. His life was reduced to a series of paranoid defense mechanisms. He had had enough of it and was ready for a confrontation whether or not he held the upper hand. But he would do his damnedest to try to obtain it.

Nellie was assigned the faux painting in Joyce Everly's daughter's room. She arrived at the Everly house at 10:00 A.M. in order to ensure that she would be there during the lunch hour that Mr. Everly had been taking. Cindy's room was right next to the study, so she knew she was only a short distance away from the video camera that would record the precious footage. Life was such a chess game recently for Nellie Brighton. There were people of power and privilege who occupied a specific place on the board. Their pawns were before them only to absorb the blows of society, enabling them to escape briefly and attack from another position. There were kings and queens and formidable warrior factions in everybody's army. Everyone had an agenda, and everyone had a limit that they would sacrifice to its end. Nellie felt a freedom from such complicated dualities. She wanted her life to reflect her values while they were still with her. She hoped that she could salvage the values of her co-workers as well. There was one task ahead of her that she was not looking forward to. Necessity dictated that she embraces the task with fortitude, if not enthusiasm, because the reward was much greater than the risk that was involved. The worst-case scenario was that she would actually have sex briefly with a man she cared nothing about. She had been forced to do so in prison to preserve her life. Now she may be called upon to save her freedom by the same actions. She had come a long way in the last six months both in prison and on the outside. She knew she was capable of doing things that she never would have dreamed of before. Such is the ugly side of life. Hopefully, it would become much more attractive from now on.

Nellie finished applying the base coat in Cindy's room around noon. Joyce Everly told her to get ready for action as her husband was expected home shortly. She thought of the irony of the situation. Here was a woman preparing her to take her clothes off with her husband. The novel *Shogun* came to mind where the Japanese women who lived by the Bushido code would arrange for concubines to keep their husband's prostate healthy. They called the moment of climax the clouds and the rain. *Very healthy.*

She was hoping her encounter would come to an end well before *any clouds* or *any raining*. She asked Joyce Everly, "It doesn't bother you that I'm going to be naked with your husband shortly?"

"Not particularly. I love my husband, but I know his eyes wander from time to time. I wouldn't be surprised to learn that other parts of him wander as well."

"Well, do me a favor and don't be late, okay?"

"Don't worry, Dear. I have impeccable timing. That's why I only have one child," she said laughing. "I think I hear him coming. Try to look sexy."

"I don't think that's going to be necessary," she said knowingly.

Chapter Nine

Kathryn Foreman lived in a very exclusive area of large riverfront homes called South Merritt Island. She had been a widow for twenty-two months after her husband was killed in a deadly avalanche. She had been devastated by her loss and found herself merely going through the motions of her life instead of actually living it. Finally, while having lunch the other day with her good friend Lucille Brooks, she resolved herself to the fact that life goes on. At least her life did despite her husband's accident. Lucille said to her, "For God's sake Kathryn get out and meet someone. You need a good lay. If you don't use that thing soon it'll dry up and blow away!"

Trying unsuccessfully not to laugh she said, "You're a dirty old woman, Lucy. I'm a *proper lady*. Do you want me to go to a meat market?"

"I want you to get laid. Whatever it takes. You have to start living your life again. James wouldn't want you locked away with your grief, would he?"

"No, he wouldn't. In fact, we talked about it. We promised each other that we would move on after an appropriate period of mourning and not look back."

"What's an appropriate period?" asked Lucille.

"I'm there, I guess."

"Well, then, what's stopping you?"

"I don't know. I guess I'm just a little out of practice. I was married for seventeen years. I'm forty years old for God's sake. That's a little old for dating."

"You look like you're thirty, Honey, and you're never too old for dating. Why don't you call a Jack? Just to get your feet wet. Or maybe something else wet before it blows away."

"God, you're awful," laughed Kathryn. "What the hell is a Jack?"

"They're very attractive men that do all the trades. Haven't you seen the white trucks around town with the playing card on the door?"

"What makes you think they do *that* kind of playing?" she asked.

"Oh, you know - you hear things from time to time. That is *if you get out* once-in-a-while!"

"You mean that they're studs for hire?"

"Not exactly, but I've been told that they're very sexy men."

"You've been told?" she asked with a doubtful look in her eye.

"All right, I fucked one of them. And it was glorious, okay?"

Kathryn started laughing so hard that her iced tea was about to come out of her nose. Then she started coughing while still laughing.

"What's so funny for God's sake? Women have needs, too. Especially if you're married to Herbert Brooks. He's only given me a couple of good rides, and I have two lovely daughters to show for it."

Kathryn started laughing again. Lucille started patting her on the back - so she didn't choke to death on the tea and said, "For Heaven's Sake, Kathryn. Try getting with the twenty-first century once in a while," said her friend.

"So, what's my excuse for hiring a Jack?" asked Kathryn.

"I don't know, knock a few of your screens out. Or better yet, take a knife and shred a few and say the cat did it."

"I don't have a cat."

"Then get a cat. Jesus, Kathryn. Do I have to do everything for you? Would you like me to buy your condoms for you?"

"Oh, would you?" she asked pleadingly. She was only half kidding.

"Forget it. Get your own. At least you don't have to hide yours. Could you imagine what Herb would say if he found mine?"

"What do you mean?" asked Kathryn.

"I had my tubes tied, remember?"

"So, what do you need the condoms for?" she asked.

Lucille Brooks just sat there looking at her for about ten seconds before she said simply, "We have to talk."

~

Bill Everly was pleased to see the white Camry with the Hands logo sitting in his driveway. He knew that meant that Nellie Brighton was doing Cindy's room. Any excuse to take in her looks was a worthwhile endeavor. He would have to examine her work *very carefully*. When he walked through the service door from the garage to the kitchen, he found his wife Joyce preparing to leave by grabbing her purse, keys and sunglasses off the counter. She told him, "I have to run out, Bill. I made some tuna for you. It's in the fridge. I'm getting my hair highlighted by Karen."

"No problem, Sweetie. I think I can make myself a sandwich."

"Thanks. Nellie's doing Cindy's room. See if she'd like a sandwich too, would you?"

"I'll take care of it," he said as his wife closed the door behind her.

Nellie pressed the remote-control record button inside her purse when she heard Bill Everly coming down the hallway. He walked in to Cindy's room and said, "You've done it again."

Thinking that he was talking about the nice job she was doing she said, "Do you like it?"

"Oh yeah," said Everly. "But I wasn't talking about the room. When I said that you've done it again, I meant stolen my heart."

"Oh, Mr. Everly," said Nellie shyly. "I did not."

"Oh, yes, you did," he said wrapping his arms around her.

"Mr. Everly," exclaimed Nellie. "What would your wife say?"

"My wife's not here," said Bill Everly. "How do you like older men?" he asked her still holding onto her. He felt himself getting excited and pressing into her from behind.

"You're not old. I mean you're older than I am, but you're not really old." She was doing the best dumb cheerleader act she had ever seen.

"I'm old enough to know what to do with a beautiful woman. Let me show you my study."

Oh, this is just too easy. What did Joyce say to him, "By the way, show the girl your study?"

They entered his study, and Nellie walked across the room to position herself away from the A/C duct where the camera was recording them. Everly walked up to her and said, "You're very beautiful, Nellie."

"Thank you, Mr. Everly."

"I'd like to see how beautiful you are without your clothes," he said heavily.

"I'd like to show you, but what if your wife catches us?"

"Why don't you just relax and let me worry about my wife," he said.

"Whatever you say," she said.

Everly walked up to her and put his hands on her breasts. "You have wonderful breasts," he said.

"I'm glad you think so."

"Take your shirt off, Nellie."

"You're sure your wife isn't coming back?" she asked.

"I'm sure."

"Well, okay." Nellie lifted her shirt over her head and threw it onto a leather chair nearby. Everly reached around behind her back and undid the clasp. Her bra fell away revealing her firm shapely breasts. Everly was lost in his lust at this point. He fumbled with his pants and finally stepped out of them. His excitement was barely visible through the slit in his boxer shorts. He caressed her nipples with his thumbs and index fingers and said, "Touch me, Nellie."

Nellie reached down and held him in her hands. *Joyce, where are you?*

"Oh, that feels so good," said Everly.

Any time now Joyce.

"My God, you're beautiful. Take off your pants!" said Everly about to explode.

Nellie undid her pants and pulled down the zipper. She slid them past her waist and Everly reached down and placed his hand against her panties. *Joyce! If you're not here in two seconds I'm gonna'* . . .

"Bill." They heard her voice.

"Oh, shit." whispered Everly fiercely. He quickly pulled his pants back up nearly catching himself in the zipper. Nellie was trying not to laugh when he whispered, "I knew this would happen."

Everly had turned ghost white. He was fully dressed in less than fifteen seconds and out the door of the study. He quickly entered Cindy's room. He straightened his clothes just as Joyce entered the room, "Bill? Are you okay?"

"I'm fine, Honey. What's up? Did you forget something?"

"The stupid coupon. I have a half-off coupon. It'll save me forty bucks."

"Good for you," said Everly.

"Did you get a sandwich?" she asked.

"No, but I'm just about to."

"Where's Nellie?" she asked.

"She's checking out the woodwork in the study. The young man did a pretty nice job."

"Well, gotta' go," she said. When she passed the study Everly could hear her say, "Bill will make you a sandwich if you get hungry, Nellie."

"Thanks, Mrs. Everly," yelled Nellie from the study. When Everly walked back in the study Nellie was fully dressed and sitting in the leather armchair. She said to Everly, "I told you that we shouldn't be fooling around. If I get caught, I'll lose my job. I need this job so if you'll excuse me, I'll finish doing your daughter's room."

"Wait a minute. We were having a good time here. She's gone now I promise. Take off your clothes again."

"Not a chance, Mr. Everly. I told you. I need this job." She stormed out of the room. It was fortunate that Bill Everly couldn't see the smirk on her face.

~

Lucille Brooks took her friends shoulders in her hands and looked her straight in the eye. "I can't believe what you just asked me, Kathryn. Haven't you ever heard of safe sex?"

"Of course, I have. I'm not a fool, Lucy."

"Well, you just sounded like one. Listen to me. I want you to promise me that you will never-ever-ever have intercourse with a man who isn't wearing a condom. Do you understand?" she said shaking Kathryn Foreman slightly.

"I hate those things."

"Do you understand?" she demanded shaking her harder.

"Okay, okay I get it."

"You *will* get it if you don't do what I say. It's a whole different world out there than it was when you and James were dating. I'm not just talking about AIDS. There's hepatitis B, herpes, genital warts, the clap, Christ even syphilis is making a comeback. It's deadly out there, honey, and you have to protect yourself."

"I said okay, Lucy. I'll be careful."

"Extra careful?"

"Extra careful."

"Good. I probably just saved your life."

"So, tell me. What's the name of your Jack?" asked Kathryn.

"Oh, no, you don't. Get your own," said Lucille.

Chapter Ten

The next day Jay West arrived at the Everly home at nine o'clock sharp. Joyce met him at the door, "Right on time."

"I take it your husband's gone?"

"Yes, he is. Did you bring another tape?"

"Certainly."

"Is there any way we could see the one they made?"

"I'm afraid not," he lied. "I don't have a conversion cartridge. But Nellie said nothing happened."

"I'm sure it didn't. I just wanted to see the look on Bill's face."

"Sorry," said Jay. He wanted to see the look on Everly's face also. But he wouldn't view the tape unless Nellie wanted to share it with him. She was sticking her neck out to help him, so he decided to respect her privacy.

Jay called Nellie on her cell phone, "We're good to go."

"You got the tape?" asked Nellie.

"Sure do," said West.

"Did you look at it?"

"What do *you* think?" he asked.

"I'm not sure *what* to think."

"Well, then *I'm* not sure what to say."

"Suit yourself, Jay. When do I get it?"

"I'm on my way, Sir?" he said sarcastically.

"I'll be glad when all of this shit is over with."

"Does that mean us, too?"

"I'm not sure what that means, Jay. I'm very tired."

"I'll be there in a minute."

West drove up to Nellie's apartment and got out of his truck, but left it running. It was a clear message to Nellie that she had insulted him and that those kinds of expressions can go two ways. When she opened the door, he handed her the tape and said, "Here. You'll have to make a couple of stills to show Everly to get him to play ball." He turned around and started walking down the concrete stairwell.

"Jay?" she said uneasily.

"What?" he asked.

"How am I supposed to do that?"

"I don't know. Take it to a photo lab."

"You know I can't do that. "Can't you help me?"

"I might see your tits. Couldn't have that, could we," he declared.

"Come on, Jay. Please don't turn on me now."

"Look, Nellie. I never looked at the tape as much as I wanted to. I respected your privacy. I know that sounds weird considering what I did to you in the past. But I had no control over that. I have control of this situation, and I chose to do the decent thing. I didn't look at the tape, but you managed to gross me on it anyway."

"I'm sorry, Jay. I've just got a whirlwind of emotions right now. I'm not acting like myself. If you want to take the tape and make the stills, I would appreciate it very much."

"Sure. No problem." He took the tape back from her and said, "My trucks running. I'll see you later." He descended the stairs, two at a time, and jogged to his truck. He got in the cab and slammed the door, "Fuck!" he said punching the steering wheel.

~

Tommy Harp had been a Jack for two years, and Hand never even tried to bring him into the stable. When Susan got the call from Kathryn Foreman, Hand sent Tommy because he didn't see the future in trying to blackmail a single woman. When Tommy picked up his work order, he asked Susan, "What's the job?"

"She didn't specify other than screen repair. You'll need a hundred feet of black flat spline and a thirty-foot roll of five-foot charcoal stock."

"You're good, Susan," he said.

"That's why they pay me the big bucks," she said facetiously.

Tommy Harp drove to Kathryn Foreman's home on Merritt Island at ten o'clock in the morning. She scheduled him for a four-hour block of time, so he knew he had plenty of daylight. When he knocked on her door, Kathryn answered in a one-piece bathing suit with a white oxford button down shirt tied at the waist, "Hello there. Are you my Jack?" she asked.

"Yes, Mrs. Foreman. My name's Tommy Harp, and I'm your Jack," he said.

"Well, Mr. Harp. I seem to need a little screen repair. Let me show you to the porch."

"You can call me Tommy," said Harp.

"Only if you'll call me Kathryn," she said.

Chapter Eleven

J ay West took Nellie's tape home and downloaded the footage into his computer. He viewed it from beginning to end one time to determine which stills he might like to produce. He decided to use the moment when Everly had his hands on Nellie's breasts. West had never touched her, and he found himself envious of the pitiful old fool. His hands had touched her, and she had touched him as well. He imagined himself in that position and found himself excited by the thought. But circumstances were never quite right between them. He always found himself either apologizing or being embarrassed. He had never really been himself with her except for the brief time when they shared a pizza. That was the best time he had had with a woman in as long as he could remember. Somehow just being together was better than sex. Sure, there was the unspoken promise that they might have a sexual encounter some time later, but just being with her made him feel special. She was a true beauty, and he had never dated anyone like her. She seemed intelligent as well - the whole package so to speak. He felt a little guilty clicking frame by frame through her video with Everly. He stopped himself and printed the three stills that he had chosen. They would be enough. He deleted the footage from his hard drive and placed the stills with the tape in an envelope for Nellie. When he tried to go to sleep that night, he reached the unmistakable conclusion that he had fallen hard for her. Probably just another pleasure the world would deny him. He was getting used to it by now.

Chapter Twelve

Tommy Harp and Kathryn Foreman worked together on her screened porch.

"You don't have to help me Kathryn," he said. "It's hot out here. Why don't you go back inside and relax?"

"You don't want me with you, Tommy?" she asked.

"No, it's not that. It's just that I want you to be comfortable."

"I am, Tommy. This is fun for me. I used to help my husband do these kinds of things all the time. I miss it."

"Well, if you're sure," he said.

"I'm sure."

They finished screening the porch and Tommy said to Kathryn, "Thanks for the help, Kathryn. I think we did a very nice job."

"That we did, Tommy. That we did. It is hot work, though. Would you like to take a swim with me?" she asked.

"Sure. That sounds great," he said. The two of them put away the tools and threw away the excess screen and spline. Kathryn untied her shirt and slipped it over her head. She could see that her perspiration had soaked through her suit in a few places and revealed the shape of her body. The fact that Tommy was taking note was not lost on her. She was proud of her body. At forty years of age, she still had tight abdominal muscles and firm buttocks. She worked out regularly and watched her weight. She was also well aware of the shape he was in. While they were working together, she discovered that he had a very nice body as well. She wasn't fooling herself. She knew very well why he was there. The screens were in perfect condition yesterday. She wondered what she might have to break tomorrow.

After their swim Kathryn said to Tommy, "How about some lunch?"

"Kathryn, you're spoiling me," he said.

"Yes, I am, and it's fun for me. I haven't spoiled a man in a while."

"Well, I'd love something to eat if it isn't too much trouble."

"No trouble at all. I'll call you when it's ready. Just relax."

Kathryn went into her house and took off her bathing suit. She changed into a white terrycloth robe that tied at the waist. There was a chicken salad in the refrigerator that she had bought earlier at a gourmet deli along with some large slices of Jewish Rye bread. She made a large sandwich with the chicken salad and added some crisp lettuce and just a hint of horseradish. The sandwich was large enough for both of them, so she cut it in half and divided it among two plates. She got two Harp Lagers from the refrigerator and put them on the kitchen table. Tommy was still out on the porch by the pool. He was drying himself off with a towel that she had draped over the patio furniture for him. When she went to the sliders, she slid them open and said, "Tommy. I just happen to have a beer with your name on it."

"My favorite. What a pleasure!"

"The pleasure's all mine," she said. "Come on in and sit down at the table."

"My shorts are still wet," he said.

"I'll get you some dry ones. Wait there." Kathryn went to her bedroom and came back with a pair of her late husband's shorts. She didn't know why she had hung on to them. Perhaps in the back of her mind it was for an occasion just like this. She returned to Tommy and said, "Try these. I think they'll fit."

"Thanks, Kathryn," said Tommy. He waited briefly until she turned around and then slid his shorts off and put the dry ones on. When he looked up, he noticed that she was obviously watching him change his shorts. Her brazen behavior kind of turned him on.

"I hope you like chicken salad," she said. "I kind of spiced it up a little,"

"Sounds great," he said. "And I really love this beer."

They ate their sandwiches and talked a lot of small talk about music and movies and how each other got their kicks. Tommy was a little sad to learn that Kathryn hadn't gotten out much lately. Finally, he asked, "So what happened to your husband?"

"He died, I'm afraid," she said numbly.

"Oh, man that's tough," said Tommy.

"Well, life goes on, Tommy," said Kathryn.

"Yeah, I guess so," he agreed. "So, what now?" he asked.

"What do you mean?" she asked rising from the table. She picked up their lunch plates and placed them in the sink.

"Well, the screens are all done. What do you want to do next?"

She untied her robe and slipped it off her shoulders. When it reached the floor, she was standing before him completely naked and said, "Well, I guess you'll just have to make love to me."

Chapter Thirteen

J ay West brought the envelope back to Nellie the next morning. She asked him in for coffee and he accepted. "So, how'd you do?" she asked.

"See for yourself," he said motioning to the package on the table. "I did three stills. You'll probably never need the tape, but it's there anyway."

"These are pretty good," she said. "I can definitely see his face. That's important."

"He's got his hands all over you. That's what's important," said West.

"You sound a little jealous, Jay. Is that what I'm hearing?"

"I've never had my hands on you even though I had a hell of an opportunity."

"I know that, Jay. So, what should we do now? Rip our clothes off and go at it like animals?"

"Don't tease me, Nellie," said West.

"You're serious, aren't you? You're getting all weepy eyed and pining for me," she ridiculed. "Well, let me tell you something, Buddy. I'm the wrong girl next door. I've been to prison. I've been somebody's bitch for God's sake. When she wanted sex, I gave her sex, whether I wanted to or not. It's called survival, Pal, and it isn't pretty. Now do you think you still want me to be your sweetheart?"

He walked toward her, and she could see that he had tears in his eyes. He didn't say anything at first, but just held out his arms in front of her. She fell into them crying. Neither of them was sure how long they stood there holding each other silently with their tears running together on their shirts.

Chapter Fourteen

Tommy Harp was lying on his back and trying to catch his breath in Kathryn Foreman's bed. "I don't think I've ever experienced anything like that," he said between breaths.

"You've never made love, Tommy?" she teased.

"Not like that. Jesus Christ, where did you learn how to do those things?"

"I just wanted to please you, Tommy. Is that so bad?"

"It's fine with me, Kathryn. I just wasn't ready for it, that's all."

"Next time, I'll try to be a little gentler," she said teasing.

"Next time?" he asked.

"Well, sure. There's a lot of work to be done around here. Can't you see that?"

"Definitely," he said.

"I might need you two or three times a week," she said caressing his chest.

"At least," he agreed. "This place is a mess."

Chapter Fifteen

When Nellie checked in with Susan at the operations desk she was told that Joyce Everly called and said she needed her back.

"I know, I didn't finish her daughter's room yesterday."

"Will one more block do it?" asked Susan.

"It should," she said. "But it's a big room, and I don't have any help."

"There's a Jack on the property this morning. If he finishes his assignment, you can have him."

"A Jack?" asked Nellie.

"Joyce Everly asked for Jay West to switch out a dishwasher and a water heater."

"Okay, thanks," she said.

"Oh, by the way. Mr. Hand wants to see you."

Nellie walked to Hand's office and knocked on the door.

"Come in," said Hand.

She opened the door and walked inside. Hand was sitting at his desk. He said to her, "When do I get my tape of Everly?"

"Very soon. I'm working there today. You can get a Jack to extract it tomorrow."

"Good. That's all. You can go."

"What about the evidence against me?"

"When I get the tape, you get your evidence."

She left without saying another word. She had a busy day ahead of her. She had to get Bill Everly to go along with the plan. Still, it shouldn't be too hard considering how much he likes to take his clothes off. She picked up her work order from Susan and headed over to the Everly's. When she got there, Joyce said, "Bill will be home about the same time as yesterday. How long do you need to make your pitch?"

"Not long. If he thinks I'm going to show you the tape, he should be willing to play along. Besides, didn't you tell me that Hand has always been a thorn in his side?"

"He sure has. The man is a menace to society in all respects. I'm surprised no one has killed him so far."

"That's a little harsh, isn't it?" asked Nellie.

"I've considered it," she said matter-of-factly.

"I just want to get this whole business over with, that's all."

"Well, I'm going out until about one o'clock. You have to make Bill come around by then. Tell him that I've agreed to make a fake video giving Jay head. He'll just edit it out before you give the tape to Hand."

82

"Okay, I guess that'll work. Were you ever caught on tape with Jay?" asked Nellie.

"No, that's not what it was all about," she said.

"I know," said Nellie. "Hand told me what it was all about."

"Well, let me tell you something that even Hand doesn't know. But you have to keep it just between us for now, okay?"

"Okay," said Nellie.

"You have to promise me with all your heart because if it gets back to Hand then I'm history."

"Okay, I promise. What is it?" asked Nellie.

"Jay's semen isn't on that girl's panties. It's Bill's semen."

"You're kidding?" asked Nellie suddenly getting the picture.

"I could never let someone be set up like that. Bill has a ton of alibis and semen is semen, right. Who could tell the difference?"

"You're pretty sharp, Joyce."

"Yeah, you too, Honey. Let's just hope that Bill feels the same way."

Chapter Sixteen

hen Bill Everly came home for lunch, Nellie was standing in his kitchen to greet him, "Hello, Mr. Everly."

"Please, call me Bill."

"Okay, Bill. How're you doing?"

"I'm fine. Where's Joyce," he asked.

"She's not here, which is fortunate, because I wanted to talk to you alone."

"You wanted to talk?"

"That's right, talk."

"What about?" asked Everly.

"About yesterday. How you wanted to take me in your study."

"Too bad we were interrupted," he said. "Care to try again?"

"As a matter of fact, yes. I want to take off my clothes. And then I want you to take off your clothes. Then I'm going to lean over your leather chair and you're going to come up behind me - and pretend to make love to me."

"Pretend? Whatever for?"

"Because I want to get it on film."

"You're crazy," he said. "If my wife saw a film like that, she would take everything I have."

"I'm glad you said that. I have something to show you." She handed him the pictures.

"Oh, my God!" he said. "How did this happen?"

"I put a camera in you're A/C duct. Notice that your hands are on my breasts?"

"I can see them. What is this, blackmail?"

"No, Bill. That's exactly what I'm trying to stop. I want to make a fake sex tape with you and give it to Jackson Hand. When he tries to blackmail you, I want you to have him arrested. The tape can't damage you because your wife will be aware of it."

"My wife?"

"That's right. I've already talked to her. She's agreed to make a similar tape with Jay West. She's going to fake having sex with him, too. His back will be to the camera, so it will be easy to fake."

"What if I refuse?" he asked knowing the answer.

"I'm sorry, but if you refuse, then I'm going to give the tape I made to your wife. She knows nothing about it and if you'll go along with me, then I'll give the tape to you. Understand?"

"Why are you doing this?" asked Everly.

"Mr. Hand is a bad man, Bill. He's had people killed and raped and God knows what else. He's blackmailing dozens of people every day. I want all his dirty little evidence confiscated, and I want him to go to prison for a long time."

"Joyce said she'll go along with this?"

"Absolutely. She's as anxious as us to put Hand away. He's a very bad man, Bill. Will you do it?"

"What choice do I have?"

"Very little, I'm afraid. When will Joyce be home?" asked Nellie for effect.

"Soon I think."

"You must have been pretty desperate to set me up like you did."

"I stand to go back to prison unless I give him a tape he can use to blackmail you. If I give him a fake tape, he can't hurt you with it, and I can still get the damning evidence against me."

"You seem to have thought this out pretty well. What would you have done if my wife hadn't interrupted us?" asked Everly.

"I guess I would have fucked your brains out," lied Nellie. "I don't want to go back to prison."

"Too bad," said Everly. "My wife has the worst timing."

Actually, Nellie thought that it was pretty damned good.

Joyce came in a short time later, and Jay West was with her. She asked her husband, "Did Nellie spell out her plan to you, Bill?"

"Yes, she did."

"And?"

"I'm game," he said.

"I thought you would be. You get to take your clothes off with a pretty young girl, you randy old goat."

"Have a care, Dear. I'm a randy middle-aged goat."

"Jay, do you have to set up the camera?" she asked.

"Yeah, but it'll only take me a minute. Who's going to go first?"

"Might as well be us, Bill. Are you ready?"

"I guess so. Do you want to watch, Joyce?" he asked.

"No, thank you, Bill. I'll give you your privacy," she said.

"Thank you, Honey."

Nellie and Bill Everly followed Jay into the study. After he set up the camera, he told them, "Now there's audio on this tape as well, so you guys are going to have to do some acting."

"No problem," said Nellie, "but could you wait for us outside? This is kind of embarrassing."

"Sure. I understand. Joyce and I will go for a walk around the block."

When they were alone, Nellie and Bill Everly went through a dialogue very similar to the one they had the day before. When Nellie was naked, she leaned over Everly's leather chair with the back obscuring all but their faces. Everly pretended to take her from behind. When he began thrusting against her, Nellie was pleased to realize that he only pretended to take down his underwear. She was also appreciative that he had his hands wrapped around her stomach and that he was not aroused. She played her part well by moaning rather loudly in concert with his thrusting pelvis. When it came time to climax, Everly pretended to pull out of her and deliver his seed on her back. Nellie in turn pretended to feel it. Everly then actually did take off his underpants, and appearing to pick them up, he went through the motions of using them wipe both of them off. When they walked off camera, they were both very naked and appeared to be spent as well.

A short time later Jay West and Joyce Everly came back and found Nellie and Bill sitting on the couch like nothing ever happened.

"Well, how did it go?" asked Joyce.

"Pretty well, I think," said Nellie. "We might want to look at the tape to make sure it looked like the real thing."

"Good idea," said Jay. "Do you want us to watch it too?"

"I don't care," said Nellie. "Do you, Bill?"

"I guess not, but it is kind of embarrassing," he said.

"Oh, nonsense," said Joyce. "We've all seen sex tapes before and most of those are fake as well."

Jay rewound the tape and played it on the television set in the Everly's living room.

When it was over Joyce said, "I think it was very good. If I didn't know better, I'd swear you were doing it."

"Me, too," said Jay.

"Well, that's what we were shooting for," said Nellie.

"You're a very beautiful woman, Nellie," said Joyce.

"Thank you."

"Yes, she is," said Jay.

"Thank you, too," said Nellie.

"Do Jay and I need to make a tape too?" asked Joyce.

"Maybe not," said Jay. "The one tape might be enough."

"All we have to do is have him arrested and his files will be confiscated," said Nellie.

"When do you think he'll contact me?" asked Bill.

"As soon as he gets the tape. You have to hire Jay back tomorrow so he can remove the tape from the study," said Nellie.

"Just make it a call-back. Say that the water heater I installed sprung a small leak. They'll send me back to redo the fitting."

"Sounds good," said Joyce.

"Well, if we're not going to make any more tapes, I guess we'll be going," said Nellie. "Come on, Jay. I'll let you buy me dinner."

"Best offer I've had all day." And then Jay added graciously, "Or at least one of them." He looked at Joyce and smiled.

Chapter Seventeen

J oyce Everly called Jacks and Hands the next morning to report a leak in her water heater.

"I'm surprised," said Susan. "Didn't Jay West do that job for you?"

"Yes," said Joyce.

"He's one of our very best Jacks. He rarely gets call-backs."

"Well, I'm sure it's not a big deal. It's just a small leak really."

"Well, I'll get someone out there right away."

"I was planning on going to the library some time this morning. Tell Jay if I'm not here the sliders around back will be unlocked, Susan," said Joyce.

"It won't be Jay, Mrs. Everly. He's on another call."

"Oh? I hate to be a bother," she said starting to worry if she were going to be caught in a lie. *What if a Jack showed up and didn't find a leak?*

"It's no bother," said Susan. "I'll get someone out there soon."

"Thanks," said Joyce.

She hung up the phone and said, "Shit. Now what?" She called her husband at the office, "Bill, we've got a slight problem."

"We do?" he asked.

"They're sending another Jack to fix the leak. Jay's on another call."

"So, what's the problem?" he asked.

"There's no leak, remember?"

"Oh, I see your point. Well, make one."

"What do you mean?" she asked.

"Just create a leak. You can do it by loosening the packing nut," he said.

"I don't know what you're talking about," she said.

"Okay, I'll walk you through it. Go into the garage and open my toolbox."

Joyce went to the garage and found her husband's toolbox on the workbench.

"I've got it," she said.

"Good. Now find a small crescent wrench or a pair of pliers."

"What's a crescent wrench?" she asked.

"It's an adjustable wrench that has a little wheel that you turn to make it bigger or smaller."

"Okay, got it," she said.

"Now go over to the water heater," he said.

"I'm there," she said.

"There should be a valve on the cold-water pipe that comes out of the wall. See it?"

"Yes, I see it."

"Good. Now turn it off."

"It's off," said Joyce.

"Now you can loosen the packing nut. It's right below the handle on the valve. Just put the wrench on the left side and pull toward you half a turn."

Thirty seconds went by and Joyce came back and said, "Okay, now what?"

"That's it. You're done," said Bill.

"But there's still no leak," she said worriedly.

"There will be when you turn the valve back on," he said. "Go ahead and do it."

Joyce turned the valve back on and sure enough a small leak began to drip from the bottom of the valve. She then said, "Well, what do you know? There's a leak."

"I'm great at breaking things," said Bill. "I just can't fix them, that's all."

"You're better at it than you think."

"Thank you, Joyce. I got to' go."

Chapter Eighteen

J oyce didn't have to go to the library, but she decided to anyway to give the Jack an opportunity to remove the camera from the study. When she came back home, she found him in the garage. She got out of her car and said, "Do you see what I mean? I put a pot under it to catch the water."

"All fixed, Mrs. Everly. It was just the packing nut. Sometimes they loosen up when you change out a water heater. It's nothing, and, of course, there's no charge."

Joyce noticed his name embroidered on his overalls and said, "Thank you, Sam."

"You're welcome. If you have any more problems just give us a call," said Sam.

"Thanks, I will," she said carrying her groceries into the kitchen. When she heard his truck drive away, the first thing she did was go into the study to examine the A/C register covering the duct. She stepped up on a chair and looked inside. It was empty. *Very interesting.* She learned that Sam was part of Jackson Hand's stable of dangerous Jacks and that he looked an awful lot like Jay West. They both had the same blond hair and mustache and were roughly about the same age and build. *All those toe-headed*

94

surfers look alike anyway, she thought. *Was Sam the one who raped that poor little girl?* Joyce Everly began to shiver with the thought of it. It was yet another reason to hope for the success of Nellie's plan.

Chapter Nineteen

The next time that Tommy Harp showed up at Kathryn Foreman's home, he saw that a Jack's truck was already in her driveway. *What the hell?* She had called Susan and asked for Tommy specifically. He wondered what the mix-up was. When he thought about another Jack being with Kathryn, he was surprised to learn that it ruffled his feathers. *Wasn't this just a job? Was he starting to have feelings for her?* He decided that he indeed was. When Kathryn met him at the door, he jerked his thumb toward the other Jack's truck and said, "What's *he* doing here?"

"That's Sam Weller," she said amused at his jealousy. "*He's* replacing the boards on the dock. *You're* taking me to the beach. Is that all right with you?" she asked teasing.

"Sure, that's fine. For a minute there I thought I was being replaced."

"Don't cut yourself short, Tommy. People can never be replaced. You're not replacing James. I'm with you because I want to be with you. Understand?"

"Yes, Kathryn. I'm sorry."

"Forget it," she said. "Let's go have some fun."

Kathryn and Tommy went from Merritt Island to a south beaches community called Aquarina. She and her husband James bought a townhouse there on the ocean where they could get away from the river and play some golf. Tommy noticed when the garage door went up that they had their own golf cart.

"Must be tricky getting that thing across A1A," he said.

"Oh, it's not that bad. Do you play?"

"Sure, a little. I'm not very good, but I like it."

"I haven't played in a long time," said Kathryn. "In fact, I haven't done a lot of things in a long time."

"It all comes back," said Tommy. "It's like riding a bicycle."

"Oh, it's a lot more fun than that." said Kathryn.

"Are you any good?" he asked.

"You seemed to think so yesterday," she said.

Realizing what she was doing, Tommy laughed and said, "I thought we were talking about golf."

"There's a time for everything, Honey. Wanna' go for a swim?" she asked.

"Sure, why not? Have you got a boogey-board?"

"As a matter of fact, I do, but there're no waves out there this time of year."

"Bring it anyway," he said with a twinkle in his eye.

Chapter Twenty

J udy Arnold was Joyce Everly's lover. She lived with her husband and two daughters in a large South-American style house overlooking the Atlantic. The house was bright white and looked like a series of huge building blocks with many sharp angles to the stucco finish. Judy was generally a carefree, happy person, but since being caught on tape with Joyce Everly, she hadn't been able to sleep through a single night. At first pills helped her a little, but she stopped taking them when she almost had a car accident taking her daughters to school. She knew that the pills were making her dopey in the morning. She figured it was better to take the girls after not sleeping very well, and then try to catch a nap later during the day. She was miserable. Joyce was afraid that she was in danger of becoming suicidal, which made for a constant source of her growing hatred for Jackson Hand. She finally was beginning to realize that she was serious when she said she had considered killing him. Nellie was not far behind her in considering it as well. Joyce knew that she and Nellie were not alone in that regard. There were probably dozens of people who would breathe easier the day Jackson Hand stopped breathing. He was evil. It was much more than greed that motivated him to do his dirty deeds. He seemed to get a sick satisfaction out of ruining people's lives. It was only a matter of time before he would meet his end. She wouldn't be a bit surprised if it happened to be an ugly one. Her dark fantasies were interrupted by a phone call, "Hello," she said.

"I miss you, Sweetheart," said Judy Arnold.

"I miss you, too. Are you alone?" asked Joyce.

"Yeah, the girls are at soccer. The hardest time is when I'm alone," she said.

"We need some time together, Honey," said Joyce.

"Jeffrey is planning a weekend of bass fishing with some of the other guys on the force. They're going to up to Atlanta for three days. Could you come stay with me?"

"I'll try," she said, "but I'm going through a rather tricky time with Bill. I have so much to tell you I could just burst. But let me tell you the good news. We may be getting out of our troubles with that evil bastard, Hand."

"Oh my God, that's too much to hope for," said Judy.

"Well, go ahead and hope, Honey. There's a pretty sharp little cookie who's determined to bring him down."

"Really?" asked Judy.

"Really. She's smart and she's brave," said Joyce.

"Sounds like you," said Judy.

"Oh, no. She's much smarter than me."

"So how *is* Bill, anyway?" asked Judy.

"Do you really care?"

"Of course, I do. You *know* I like Bill, I'm just a little jealous of him."

"Well, he's fine. Let me tell you what's been happening. Hand pressures this girl to get a blackmail tape he can use against Bill. Well, you can imagine how hard it is to get Bill out of his pants. That's like saying to the wolf, *would you like to chase the chickens?* Anyway, she gets him to drop his drawers but has arranged beforehand for me to almost catch them in the act."

"Why in the world would she do that?" asked Judy.

"To blackmail Bill into helping her with her plan."

"Which is?"

"She wants to make a fake sex tape to trap Hand in his blackmail scheme. She needs the tape to get back some damning evidence against her. She doesn't want to make a real blackmail tape, so she decides to make a fake one that I'm well aware of. We were all sitting there in our living room saying, *'Okay you two take off your clothes and we'll walk around the block, so you don't have to be embarrassed.'* Can you imagine?"

"That's amazing." said Judy.

"Yeah, well Bill's happier than a pig in shit because he gets to take off all of his clothes with a beautiful girl. It was all pretty innocent, but it looked real as hell."

"So, Bill thinks that he's saving his ass when actually he might be saving both of ours," said Judy.

"You got it. I told you she was smart."

"Well, God bless her. I'll say a prayer for us. Please try to get over to see me. Peter leaves on Friday. Friday till Monday. Tell Bill that I'm really depressed and that I need a friend. You'd only be telling the truth. Just don't tell him that there's only one bed to make in the morning."

"I'll try, Sweetheart. I gotta' go. I'm making dinner."

"I miss your cooking as much as your body," said Judy.

"*Good-bye*. Love you."

"I love you, too."

Chapter Twenty-one

When Nellie went to the office the next day, Susan gave her a catering assignment and told her that Hand wanted to see her in his office. *This is getting tiresome.* She walked down the hall past the bathroom and tried Hand's office door without knocking. The door was unlocked, but the office was empty. Thinking that Hand might be in his bathroom she called out, "Mr. Hand?" There was no answer. She walked out of the office and back down the hallway toward the front door. When Susan saw her coming, she said, "Oh, he's not in yet. He said he wants you to wait for him."

"I'm going to go across the street for a latte."

"Suit yourself," said Susan. "Oh, by the way, was Jay West any help to you the other day at the Everly's?"

"What?" asked Nellie not knowing where this was going.

"With your faux painting. Was Jay any help?"

"Oh, yeah. Jay's a really good worker," she said.

"He's pretty cute, too. Don't you think?"

"I've never thought about it. I have a boyfriend," Nellie lied.

"Well, I'd never kick him out of bed," said Susan.

"I'll tell him you said so," said Nellie.

"Don't you dare," said Susan half-heartedly.

"Do you want anything from Starbuck's?"

"Been there, done that," said Susan.

When Nellie walked out of the office, she saw Jay West just pulling up. She rushed over to his truck and said, "This is our chance. He's out of the office and his door is open -unlocked. I was just there and saw it. It's open. Do you have the bug?"

"Yeah, I've got it. Is Susan in the office?"

"Uh huh. I just left her. She's got the hots for you."

"I don't see how that helps us," he said seriously. He thought for a minute and then walked over to Susan's white Toyota Camry. He took out his keys and made a series of ugly scratches in the paint. Then he said to Nellie, "Give me twenty seconds and then come running in with the bad news."

Jay walked quickly over and entered the front entrance to Jacks and Hands. When he got inside, he approached Susan's desk and said, "Good morning, pretty lady. Mind if I use your bathroom?"

"Help yourself," said Susan.

Nellie looked at her watch briefly and then followed him in. When she got through the door she said, "Susan! Someone keyed your car."

"Shit," said Susan getting up and running out the door. Nellie followed her.

Jay came out of the bathroom and went directly to Hand's office. He quickly went in and shut the door. The first thing he did was place a small microphone underneath Hand's desk. Then he went to the safe and tried the handle. He couldn't believe his incredible luck as it opened easily. Hand must have forgotten to spin the dial the last time he closed it. He removed a number of large envelopes, VCR tapes and DVDs. He noticed that the safe was a Diebold variable number setting model, so he reset the numbers and closed it back up. Taking off his shirt he filled it with all of the envelopes and tapes. He was about to walk out of Hand's office when he heard them coming through the front door. Hand was followed by teary-eyed Susan Cole and Nellie Brighton trying to console her. Hand was saying, "Who you piss off is your business, Susan. I'm not going to pay for a new paint job on your car."

"It probably won't cost all that much," said Nellie. "Maybe they can just touch it up." Nellie noticed the door to Hand's office just closing as he started down the hall.

"*I CAN'T STAND IT! I CAN'T STAND IT! I CAN'T STAND IT!*" screamed Nellie. "*I'M NOT EVEN IN CONTROL OF MY OWN LIFE ANYMORE! I WON'T GO BACK! I'LL KILL MYSELF FIRST! WANNA WATCH, JACKSON? WANNA GET IT ON TAPE? I SWEAR I*

WON'T GO BACK!" Nellie had backed herself against a wall and then slid slowly down to the floor and curled into the fetal position. She kept whispering, *"I won't go back, I won't go back..."* She rocked back and forth with a far away look in her eyes. Hand turned to Susan and said, "Would you excuse us for a minute?"

"Sure. I'll just powder my nose."

When Susan was out of the room, Hand whispered fiercely to Nellie, "Get hold of yourself for God's sake. You did your job and now you're home free."

Nellie kept rocking back and forth, *"I won't go back, I won't go back..."*

Hand was getting a little nervous. He whispered forcefully, "Nellie, snap out of it."

Nellie kept rocking back and forth and finally hand shook her shoulders and shouted, *"Nellie!"*

She focused on his face from a place very far away and said, "Mr. Hand?"

"You were hysterical, Nellie. You need to relax. Come with me," he said.

Hand led Nellie into his office. He closed the door behind them and said, "Look, Nellie. I know you've been under a lot of strain, but it's over. I got the Everly tape last night, and it's very good. I sent him a copy this morning. You did your job, and now you're home free. Do you understand?"

"Where are my pictures?" said Nellie in a sleepy voice.

Hand looked over to his safe and said, "Shit."

"What's the matter," asked Nellie.

"It's my damn safe. I've been having trouble opening it. I thought I left it open."

"When do I get my pictures, Mr. Hand?"

"Soon. Very soon." Hand tried to open the safe, but was unsuccessful.

"You're trying to trick me, aren't you, Mr. Hand."

"No, I'm not. I told you, I'm done with you."

"Can I use your bathroom, Mr. Hand?"

"Yeah, go ahead," he said.

When Nellie went into the bathroom the first thing she did was go to the window. She saw that the lock was open so she quickly locked it. *Jay must have made his escape through here.* She went to the sink and splashed water on her face making sure to *"accidentally"* wet her upper torso as well. She went back into Hands office and said, "I've kept my side of the bargain. I want you to stop fucking with me," she said with her voice rising.

"I'm not trying to do anything. It's *over.* You have nothing to worry about."

"So, you say. I want my life back," she said.

"You've got it back. I'll give you the pictures and the baggie as soon as I can open the safe."

"Why should I believe you?" she asked.

"Because it's the truth."

"Who raped that little girl, Mr. Hand?"

"What? What's that got to do with anything?"

"I just want to know what kind of slime-ball rapes a sixteen-year-old girl?"

"A very frightened slime-ball that's what kind," said Hand.

"Sam Weller is twice your size. What would he have to fear from someone like you?" she goaded.

"Who said anything about Weller?"

"He's the only Jack who could pass for Jay West. I'm guessing that he's the one you used to set Jay up."

"I like a smart girl, Nellie."

"So, tell me. Why would a guy as big as Sam Weller be worried about a guy like you?"

"Size isn't everything, Nellie. Weller's size wouldn't do him that much good in prison. You know the rules. You've been around the block. Crawford, wasn't it?"

"Yeah, I've been around. So why would Weller be afraid of you?"

"Let's just say that there's a certain gun in an evidence room with his fingerprints on it."

"A murder weapon," she said dully.

"That's right. An unsolved murder."

"But Weller never really killed anybody did he? If he did, he might be willing to turn himself in. That's the whole

107

secret behind your operation. You prey on the innocent because they have the most to lose. They can feel cheated, whereas the guilty may accept their fate."

"You're a very clever woman, Nellie."

"So where is this evidence room?" asked Nellie.

"What difference does it make, Nellie? It's ancient history."

"I'll tell you what difference it makes. *You* raped that little girl."

"You're crazy. I wasn't anywhere near where she was raped."

"But you ordered Weller to rape her. You conspired to rape a young girl. You're just as guilty as if you did it yourself."

"Weller's a weakling. He's on the way out anyway."

"You're going to send him to prison, aren't you?"

"That's a good place for him. He's become a little unstable."

"So, when do I get my pictures?" she demanded.

"As soon as I can open the God damned safe."

Chapter Twenty-two

N
ellie walked out the door of Jacks and Hands and instantly saw Jay standing next to a white van. She ran up to him and asked, "Did you get it?"

"Uh huh. It's all on tape. The guy in the van here is a tech-head. I figured this was too important to leave to an amateur," he said.

"Do you think it's enough to put him away?"

"I don't know. It doesn't really matter," said Jay.

"What do you mean it doesn't really matter?" she asked confused.

"I emptied his safe."

"Really? That's wonderful." she said excitement filling her voice. "What did you do with the stuff?"

"What stuff?" he asked blankly."

"Where is the evidence?" she asked.

"What evidence?" he asked.

"What you took from the safe?" she asked.

"What safe is that, Nellie? I don't remember any safe."

"But then the only evidence against him is the false evidence that I did with Everly."

"Strange world isn't it, Nellie. But I don't think he'll ever get to trial."

"Why not?" she asked.

"Because we just freed all of his worst nightmares."

"What do you mean?"

"Well, there are the Jacks, and then there are the Hands, and finally there are his victims."

"I think I see what you mean," said Nellie.

"He better hope your tape puts him in jail. That's the only safe place for him now."

Chapter Twenty-three

Nellie and Jay called the Everly's house from her cell phone. When Joyce answered Nellie said, "I just left Hand's office. He said he sent out the tape this morning."

"He's using the mail? I can't believe the nerve of that guy," said Joyce.

"Well, he's arrogant. It goes with the territory, I guess."

"Oh, so you're saying that all homicidal-blackmailing-asshole conspirators are arrogant? I can't believe that!" said Joyce factiously. "Well, I'm sure he didn't send it to this address. What if *I* opened it? Even *he* isn't that arrogant."

"He probably sent it to Bill's office. It'll take until tomorrow to get there," said Nellie.

"How did your tape go?" asked Joyce anxiously.

"I think we got him."

"Really?" she asked, hope filling her voice. "That's music to my ears!"

"You and a lot of other people. There's more good news," said Nellie.

"Well, tell me, girl. Don't keep me waiting."

"I think Jay got all of the dirt out of his safe."

"Oh, my God." said Joyce excitedly. *"All of it?"*

"He said he emptied it. But Hand doesn't know it yet because he changed the combination before he closed it."

"Can you find out whether Jay got my tape, Nellie?"

"I'll try. If it was in there, then he got it."

"Oh, that is just too perfect," said Joyce. "We're might be free. I can't wait to tell my sweetheart. I'll call you back, okay?"

"Okay, we'll talk to you later, Joyce."

When Nellie hung up the phone, Jay asked her, "You'll try to do what?"

"She wants to know whether her tape was in the safe."

"Good question," said Jay.

"Oh, come on. Don't tell me you destroyed all the evidence. I'm not buying it."

"It's my ass, Nellie. I'm the one who could go to jail for rape, remember?"

"Jay, listen to me. You may be totally off the hook, but you have to trust me. You have to let me look through the evidence for Joyce's tape."

"And if she gets her tape back what's her motivation to go through with the sting. They might just forget the whole thing if they think that Hand is out of business. Not everyone has the balls to step up and do their civic duty you know."

"Jay, you have to trust me. Tell me the truth. You didn't destroy the tapes, did you?"

"No, I didn't," he said.

"Thank God," said Nellie. "Where are they now?"

"I think we're playing with fire, Nellie. Those tapes aren't labeled. God knows what's on them. I don't think I want to see all that shit. It's like looking into hell. I'm not sure I'm ready for that," he said.

"Then I'll do it alone," said Nellie.

"What? You're going to look at all the tapes?"

"Not all of them. Once I find the one with Joyce and her lover, I'm done."

"I don't know, Nellie. I think we should keep Joyce guessing for a little while. At least until we find out whether they intend to follow through with the plan. Fair enough?"

"I'll go along with that, but I still want to look at the tapes. I promise I won't tell anybody about their contents without your consent. Would that be okay?"

"I guess so. I still wish you would just leave them alone until Hand goes to jail."

"I have another agenda, Jay. I'm trying to protect someone that I care about."

"Okay, I hear you," said Jay. *I just wish it was me you cared so much about.*

"So, you'll let me see them?" she asked.

"Yeah, you can see them. I'll set them up for you and then take a long walk. How's that?"

"Thank you, Jay. You won't be sorry."

"I'm already sorry, Nellie. I saw you on your first day of work. I'm partly to blame for the difference between the person you were then, and the person you are now."

"I'm not blaming you, Jay."

"You don't have to, Nellie. I can do it enough for both of us."

Chapter Twenty-four

J ay West drove to his apartment with Nellie Brighton. They set up Jay's VCR, connected to his television, in order to play the tapes and laid them all out on the coffee table. Jay showed her the basic rudiments of playing, rewinding and pausing and then he was on his way. As he got up from the couch he said, "I'm leaving, Nellie. I wasn't kidding. I don't want to see this stuff."

"I understand, Jay, but I have to. I hope I can make you understand someday."

"Just remember. Some stuff changes you. You want to get it out of your head, but there's no reset button. Once you see it, you're affected."

"I have to do this, Jay."

"So, I guess I have to let you. I'll be back in about an hour. If you see something that looks like a snuff film just stop the tape and fast forward, okay?"

"What's a snuff film?" she asked.

"Someone being killed and filmed on purpose."

"Jesus Christ," said Nellie bleakly.

"You don't have to do this, Nellie. Not for any one of those people."

"Yes, I do, Jay. Get out of here."

Jay left Nellie alone with the tapes. He prayed that he would return to the same person after his walk on the beach.

Nellie settled onto Jay's battered old couch and watched what goes on behind closed doors. Some of it was fairly mild considering the darker escapades already catalogued in her short nineteen years of life. Some of it shocked even her. What surprised her was that very little of it was pretty. Most of the sexual exploits exuded a desperation that eclipsed the very sensuality that it promised. For the most part she witnessed a feverish gluttony of the senses. Most of the players were on a hysterical mission of forbidden madness. At times the images on the tapes were completely devoid of tenderness. Other times laughter took the place of where you would otherwise expect emotion. Fortunately, she was able to discover Joyce's tape before witnessing the death of any human being. She briefly said a prayer of thanks. Having found the tape of Joyce and her lover, Nellie was rewarded by an immediate feeling of relief. Her first impulse was to fast forward past the section that incriminated Joyce for having a woman as a lover. But she lingered on the images briefly wanting to understand the nature of what a man had failed to provide for her. There was a tenderness shared between them, but she knew that wasn't the reason they sought each other's company. At last, she concluded that the time they spent together transcended sex or any other physical connection. They seemed to talk without talking. They laughed at the ironies of life only to be found in each other's company. Nellie was confident that no one else would get the joke. *Maybe that's what love is. No one else gets the joke.*

She knew that she could then assure Jay that he was no longer in danger of being connected with the rape of the girl in the theme park. She could tell him that Joyce deceived Hand by delivering Bill's genetic blueprint in place of his. She would try to make him understand that there was a good reason to keep the information from him as long as Joyce and her lover were at risk. Now he was free. Freed by information that could have been his for some time. *Would he understand?* Would *she* understand if *he* had kept similar information from her?

Hand couldn't hurt Joyce anymore. So at least that was some measure of victory. But she had to press on. She hadn't found her own tape yet. The next tape she witnessed involved a young boy. He was an early teenager with a face full of acne and a raging libido. The Hand was teasing him by coming up behind him and wrapping her hands around him. His erection was obvious. It embarrassed him at first and then she quelled his discomfort by lowering her hands and freeing him from the restriction of his clothes. Nellie knew what was coming next so she fast-forwarded the tape.

The next section involved an older man trying to stay up to the task of entering a pretty young Hand. Unfortunately, he failed miserably time and time again despite her repeated efforts to drop to her knees and expedite matters with the loving caress of her lips. Sadly, the man finally gave up, but Nellie imagined it cost him dearly just as well. Such was the content of many of the tapes. None were remarkable. Life is mostly full of private wishes. When the privacy is gone, then dignity soon follows. We are reduced to the true nature of humanity. God's work certainly, if not his best work. If she were able to put a face on all the sordid acts captured on tape that Jackson Hand chose to punish them for, it wouldn't be smiling. But it would surely have hope. Hope that someone would pay attention to it for just a short while.

Finally, she came to the section of tape where she was positioned naked on her couch with Jay West. It was the tape that the still pictures were made from that she was shown in Hand's office. She stopped the tape and examined the envelopes that were on the table. The still pictures were there. She had every reason to believe that they were all there, but that wasn't the evidence that concerned her. Inside another envelope, she found the baggie full of narcotics and the crack pipe as well. They looked exactly like the ones in the pictures. A wave of relief washed over her and she felt anxious to relieve Jay of his torment as well. His guilt was a tangible thing that he carried with him, anguished at being an unwilling instrument at the hands of Jackson Hand to compromise her hope of freedom. She couldn't wait until he returned from his walk on the beach. While she was waiting, she restarted the tape of the two of them together on her couch. The first thing that she noticed was that although he was naked, he never had an erection. She could instantly see that he was uneasy with the situation. He was very gentle whenever he came in contact with her, brushing the hair out of her eyes and caressing her cheek with the back of his fingers. There was a clear demonstration of emotion that reminded Nellie of Joyce's tape with her lover. The last thing that Nellie noted was that Jay's face was turned away from the camera for much of the time. The few times that she could see his eyes clearly, she had the distinct impression that they were holding back tears.

~

A short time later, Jay walked through the door having completed his walk on the beach. At first Nellie was startled, and then she realized that it had to be Jay. No one else would barge in without knocking. He saw her wipe a tear from her eye as she looked up and smiled to him.

"Pretty bad, huh," he said as he walked over to the refrigerator for a beer. "You want one?" he asked holding up the can.

"No, thanks," she said. "How was your walk?" was her attempt at small talk. She wasn't sure just what she should share with him at this point. Everything was moving a little too fast for her taste.

"Super," he said sarcastically. "I just got lost so you could review the tapes. So, how'd it go?" he asked again, clearly agitated by her unwillingness to broach the subject.

"I found Joyce's tape," she said, wiping another tear from her eye.

"What about your tape? Did you find the part where I took advantage of you?" he asked facetiously.

"Don't do this, Jay," she pleaded. She was heavily crying at this point and lifting her shirt to blot the tears from her eyes. "Jesus Christ, what a mess."

"So, did you find it?" he asked glaring at her.

"Yes, I found the tape of us together," she cried.

"Well, what did you think? Think we could make a good porn film together?"

"Please don't, Jay."

"Please don't what? You're the one who had to see it. You couldn't be satisfied by just destroying the damned thing, could you? You had to throw it in my face again to show me what a complete asshole I am. Does that make you feel better about yourself?"

"I don't think you're an asshole," she said with tears falling from her eyes. "No more than I am. Oh, God Jay, that bastard has me hating myself. It's just not fair. We're all victims, Jay. None of us are assholes. We're just victims. Oh, please would you just hold me for a moment - I feel so damned empty. I feel like I don't have a soul anymore." She started quaking and trying to breathe through her nose, which was heavily stuffed up. She coughed a few times and managed to say, "I need a tissue."

Jay walked her to the bathroom and pulled a few feet of toilet paper from the roll, "Here." He handed it to her. She blew her nose loudly and used the edges to wipe her eyes.

"Feel better?" he asked.

"At least I can breathe a little better."

"So, what now? Can we destroy all this shit and get it over with?"

"I've been thinking about that," she said catching her breath. "I think we have to give it back to all the victims."

"What? I don't want to get involved in anything like that. Hell, *we'll* probably get arrested for blackmail."

"I don't think so. Just think about it for a minute. What if Hand had a tape of you? Would you want me to tell you I destroyed it or would you want to receive it and destroy it yourself? Wouldn't you like to make sure that the nightmare is all over with? Just think about the relief that the victims will feel if they *receive* the damning evidence against them, free of charge. Wouldn't that be cool?"

"Yeah, I guess so, but I don't get off so easily, do I. I don't have a tape. All I have is my semen on some girl's underpants. Where's my relief, Nellie. How am I supposed to get off the hook?"

"You've been off the hook."

"What?"

"You're off the hook," she said shakily. She had to feel out the situation before she could reveal the whole truth. "There's no evidence against you, Jay."

"What are you talking about? I know that Joyce Everly delivered a semen sample to Hand. What's to stop him from making the call to the Orlando Police Department?"

"Nothing, but it's not your semen."

"What do you know, Nellie? Tell me," he said angrily.

"Don't get mad, Jay. Joyce told me that she tricked Hand, but I couldn't tell you until I knew she was in the clear. Please try to understand." She started to cry again.

"What do you mean she tricked Hand," he demanded, his voice rising with the veins in his neck.

"She gave Hand her husband's semen knowing that it could never implicate him. He has a number of alibis. She couldn't bring herself to frame you like that even though the bastard assured her that he was only going to threaten you with it. Joyce was sick to learn that the girl was raped in order to manipulate you in Hand's repulsive game. But you see why I couldn't tell you, don't you? You would have tipped your hand and then Joyce would have been punished along with her lover."

"So, you let me sweat it out, night after night, just to protect that bitch."

"I knew that you were safe, that's the important thing. I wanted to tell you, and I would have, as soon as I could trust you not to give her away."

"Well, then I guess we're even," said Jay.

"I don't blame you for what you did to me. I know you didn't have any choice in the matter."

"That's not what I meant," he said.

"What do you mean?" she asked clearly confused.

"You've been off the hook too. Your prints aren't on the baggie and the crack pipe, mine are."

"Are you serious?"

"Damn straight. I could never bring myself to frame you like that," he mimicked her comment about Joyce.

"You bastard!" her face began to turn red.

"Hey, what comes around - goes around. I thought I was doing you a favor. At least you wouldn't have gone back to prison."

"And the reason why you didn't tell me was. . . ?"

"Listen, I had a lot on the line, Honey. I wasn't going to trust you not to tell Hand to go fuck himself. Then, I would have gone to jail when he learned that I didn't really compromise you. Pretty ironic, huh?"

"I guess if we could have just trusted each other, we could have gotten a little more sleep at night."

"A lot more sleep," said Jay. "Oh, what a tangled web we weave."

"Speaking of which, what do you think we should do about Joyce and Bill Everly?"

"I guess let them off the hook, just like everyone else."

"I'm not sure that would be a very good idea."

"What do you mean?" asked Jay. "What about all the joy you want to bring to everybody?"

"Do you trust them to go ahead with the charges against Hand if they think they're off the hook?"

"I think I see what you mean," he said.

"Look, I hate the bastard, but I don't want to kill him, do you?" she asked, still a little unsure of *her own* feelings.

"I could care less," he said.

"You have to wake up every day, Jay, and look yourself in the mirror. Why don't we let the law take care of Jackson Hand? If he walks, then, the Jacks will surely kill him if one of his victims doesn't. It's like we're handing him over on a silver platter."

"It's nothing less than he deserves," said Jay. All he could think of was the poor girl who was raped just to give Hand leverage over him. People like that didn't deserve to live.

"Well, I'm going to give the system a chance to put him away. We have the tape that just about names Sam Weller," said Nellie.

"Does it? I'm not so sure. I think a good defense attorney could get him out of it in a number of ways."

"All the more reason to force Joyce and Bill to go through with it. We can't leave him out on the street. We can't turn him over to the Jacks and Hands. Our only reasonable course of action is to let Joyce think that we haven't found her tape. That's the only thing that will make her encourage Bill to pursue the blackmail charge," said Nellie with a sudden conviction she had been looking for. "I'm going to continue to turn the screws until he does the right thing. That's all I can do, and it's a hell of a lot more than that bastard Hand deserves. There's a part of me that wouldn't mind seeing him torn apart by the Jacks."

"You're kinda' cute when you're homicidal, you know that?"

Chapter Twenty-five

Jay and Nellie were sitting on his couch trying to gather their thoughts. Nellie was feeling a little calmer and had gotten a beer from Jay's refrigerator. She had destroyed the tape of her and Jay and returned the narcotics and crack pipe to the envelope for Jay to dispose of.

"I'm still pissed at you for not trusting me," she said.

"You took the words right out of my mouth," said Jay. "What are you going to tell Joyce?"

"That we're still looking at the tapes and to go ahead with the plan."

"You think they'll do it?"

"God, I hope so. We have to get rid of that sick bastard somehow. What if he were to take off and start up somewhere else? The man is evil."

"Well, make the call," said Jay.

"Right now? I haven't figured out exactly what to say yet."

"Don't over think it. Just make the call. Tell them to let us know as soon as Bill gets the tape."

"All right," she said testily. "Just let me compose my thoughts, would you?" Deception didn't come easily for

Nellie. Even though it meant taking Jackson Hand out of circulation, she hated the idea of making someone suffer any longer than they had to. She dialed the phone.

"Hello."

"Joyce, it's Nellie."

"Well? Tell me the good news," she said.

"No news yet, I'm afraid." Nellie bit her lower lip.

"You haven't found the tapes yet?"

"We have them, but we're not exactly sure what's here. There's a lot of stuff to go through," she lied. "Hand has been pretty busy for the past few years."

"Why can't you just destroy the damned stuff?" asked Joyce nervously.

"I've given it a lot of thought. I don't think that's the way to proceed."

"What the hell are you saying?"

"Calm down, Joyce. Everything's going to be fine."

"What are you trying to do, take up the operation where Hand left off?"

"You know that's not true. What a shitty thing to say, Joyce. You know I'm trying to help you, don't you?"

"I know that. I'm sorry - it's just that we're so close. *I'm* so close to having this huge cloud finally lifted off of my head, I'm crawling out of my skin."

"I know how you feel. Just give us a little more time. We'll find your tape, don't worry. Did you destroy the copy that Hand gave you?"

"Well, what do *you* think? You think I left it around for Bill to find? Of course, I destroyed it. I never even showed it to Judy."

"How's she holding up?" asked Nellie.

"She's very fragile right now. I feel like, at any time, a disappointment could . . . oh, I don't know. I'm very worried about her, so please tell me the moment you find it."

"I will. Is Bill ready to go ahead with the accusation? He's not getting cold feet or anything, is he?"

"Not as long as he thinks you'd use that tape against him. Let us know when you find your own tape, okay. Then, maybe you can take the heat off Bill."

"You don't understand, Joyce. It's not about me, or even you and your friend. It's about all of us. It's about making the world a better place to live for God's sake. Don't you realize how dangerous he is?"

"Yes, I know. I just want it to be over with, that's all."

"It will be, I promise. Call me when Bill gets the tape, okay?"

"Okay."

"First thing, right?"

"I said I would."

"Okay. Bye, Joyce."

"Bye, Nellie."

When Nellie hung up the phone she turned to Jay and said, "God, I hated doing that. It made me feel dirty inside."

"Hang in there, kid. We're at the clubhouse turn. All we gotta' do is finish the race."

"I feel so exhausted. I don't know what's the matter with me."

"Go lay down on my bed for a while. The sheets are pretty clean. I'll take the couch. I could use a nap myself."

"Are you sure?"

"Go. I'll wake you in a couple of hours."

"Thanks, Jay."

"You're welcome."

Chapter Twenty-six

Tommy Harp was picking up his assignment from Susan Cole when Jackson Hand opened his door and silently waved him down the hallway. As Tommy approached him, he said, "Do you have a minute to speak to me, Tommy?"

"Sure, Mr. Hand. What's up?"

"Please, come in my office," he said opening his door and waving his hand toward the leather chair opposite his desk. Hand walked around and sat down when Tommy had seated himself. He looked Tommy in the eye and said, "I'm afraid I might have some pretty bad news for you."

"Oh?" asked Tommy.

"It involves your friend, Mrs. Foreman."

Tommy was about to insist that he and Kathryn Foreman were merely work acquaintances when Hand said, "Relax, Tommy. It's none of my business how well you get along with our clients or in what capacity you satisfy them so to speak. I told you to treat her well, and it appears that you have. What I have to tell you involves her late husband, James."

"I don't understand," said Tommy.

"It involves a tape that I received through the mail, of all things. A rather damning piece of evidence against him as it turns out."

"He's dead, Mr. Hand. Who would want to harm a dead man's reputation? What good would that do?" asked Tommy.

"I'm sure I don't know, Tommy. All I can do is bring it to your attention since you and Mrs. Foreman are becoming such good friends. She's asked for you specifically four days in a row."

"Yes, I know. She's a very nice lady, Mr. Hand. I'd hate to see anything hurt her."

"I thought you'd say that. Perhaps I should show you the tape."

"I'm not sure I want to see it. It has nothing to do with me."

"Well, perhaps Mrs. Foreman should be forewarned so to speak . . ."

"I'll look at it, Mr. Hand. I don't think we need to involve Mrs. Foreman."

"As you wish," said Hand. He started the VCR within his bank of electronics and the television screen came to life.

Chapter Twenty-seven

The Foreman Foundation was created by Kathryn Foreman's late husband, James Foreman. It provides thirteen scholarships for low-income families that for one reason or another slip through the cracks of Florida's educational system. It was designed for students that graduate high school with a 2.0 grade point average or better, but the main criteria are the compulsory letters of recommendation.

Each applicant must have letters of recommendation from three specific areas. The first area of reference is professional, which involves either doctors or lawyers. The second is instructional, which involves former teachers and school administrators. The third reference area is spiritual, which involves a clergyman who is familiar with the past behavior of the applicant and can speak for his or her moral and religious background. The overall scrutiny of the applicant is almost as painstaking as that of a high-level security clearance applicant in the United States Army. The reason is fairly obvious. There are only thirteen scholarships, and typically there are over twelve hundred students who apply. A free college education doesn't come along very often, so it is usually taken very seriously.

Thirty-nine grateful graduates are presently a useful part of society due to the Forman Foundation, to date. Thirty-nine hard working undergraduates are soon to follow. As director of the applicant screening committee, Kathryn Foreman works very hard to perpetuate the good work set in motion by her late husband, James.

Chapter Twenty-eight

The video that Jackson Hand was running for Tommy Harp showed man with blond hair having a vigorous sexual encounter with a younger African-American female.

"Do you know what you're watching?" asked Hand.

"Don't tell me that's him?" said Tommy.

"Correct," said Hand.

"That's James Forman?" he asked incredulously.

"A rather unflattering position for the Chairman of the Foreman Foundation, wouldn't you say?"

"Who's the girl?" asked Tommy.

"One of the Foreman recipients," said Hand.

"You're not serious," said Tommy. "Who sent you the tape?"

"I haven't the slightest idea, but I'm sure it's only a copy."

"What makes you say that?" asked Tommy.

"Someone wants something."

"Wants what? Was there a note?"

"No note. Not yet, but I have a feeling I'll be receiving one sometime soon."

"Will you let me know when it comes? I'd like to help nail this bastard."

"I thought you'd say that, Tommy. I promise when I find out what this guy wants, you'll be the first to know."

"Thanks, Mr. Hand. I'm glad you showed this to me instead of Kathryn. This would destroy her and cast a horribly dark cloud on the Foundation."

"I'm just glad I could help," said Jackson Hand with a smile.

Chapter Twenty-nine

Kathryn Foreman took Tommy Harp to the Brevard Symphony Orchestra's performance of Beethoven's Pastoral Symphony. The Sixth was always her favorite, and she didn't understand why Tommy didn't seem to be enjoying himself. All evening he was fidgeting with his necktie and constantly crossing and uncrossing his legs. Finally, she asked him, "What's wrong, Tommy? You're a wreck."

"Nothing," he answered, but she didn't believe it.

"Something's bothering you. Don't you like the music?"

"It's not the music. I've always loved this symphony."

"Then, what is it? You can tell me," she said.

"Not here. Not now," he said.

"Well, all right, but I wish you could just relax. You're giving me the heebie-jeebies."

"I'm sorry, Kathryn. It's nothing. I'll be good."

"That's more like it."

Tommy couldn't get the video out of his mind. He tried to enjoy the symphony, but all he could think about was protecting Kathryn from the sick son-of-a-bitch that sent the tape to Jackson Hand. He couldn't wait to get his hands on him. How could anyone be so cruel to a widowed woman? Some people will do anything to get what they want. Later that evening, Tommy was sitting on a sofa with Kathryn back at her house on Merritt Island. The night was warm and still, and they could see the lights of Melbourne shining on the water across the river. Kathryn reached out and began massaging Tommy's neck, "Are you going to tell me what was bothering you, Tommy?"

"It's complicated, but don't worry about me. I'll figure it out."

"Tommy, stop being so mysterious. Your problems are my problems. I want to help."

"I don't want you to get involved, Kathryn. I'll handle it, *alone*."

"If you're in some kind of trouble, I think I need to know," she said.

"It's not me. I'm worried about a friend of mine, that's all."

"Should I be jealous?" she asked coyly.

"I can assure you, Kathryn, you're the only one who has my heart."

"And you have mine, Tommy. All I ask is that you think about letting me help you *or* your friend. Okay?"

"Okay. I'll think about it," he said.

Kathryn rose and took Tommy's hand and pulled him close to her. She placed his hand beneath the front of her dress and said, "Think about this."

Chapter Thirty

When Bill Everly received the tape by mail the next day, he immediately called his wife, "Joyce, it's Bill."

"You got it, didn't you?"

"It's here. He's demanding that I back away from the acquisition of the property next to Sea Oats Vistas. That would clear the way for his damned strip mall, can you believe it?"

"Nothing that slime ball does would surprise me," said Joyce. "Are you sure you're ready to go ahead with this?"

"Absolutely," said Bill.

"It could get pretty ugly, Bill," she said. Joyce still wasn't sure whether the truth about Judy Arnold would surface during the investigation. Nellie assured her that any confiscated information would be inadmissible for any application other than the prosecution of Jackson Hand. She further hoped that Jay West was able to secure the damning evidence against her and Judy so she could tell Bill that maybe they should call the whole thing off. Joyce knew that Nellie was forcing Bill's hand and was amused by his gung-ho attitude as if he were some kind of champion for justice. She knew in her heart that Hand had to be put away

139

even at the risk of exposing her relationship with Judy Arnold. She told her husband, "I'm proud of you, Bill, for seeing this thing through."

"Someone has to. I'm going to the police as soon as I hang up the phone. I'll give my statement along with Nellie's, and I expect that Hand will be picked up by nightfall."

"Do you want me to come with you?" she asked.

"I could use the support," said Bill.

"Then come and get me and we'll go down there together," she said.

"You're a good wife, Joyce. Have I ever told you that?"

"Not nearly enough," she said jokingly.

"I can't wait to get that joker off my back," he said.

If you only knew, she thought.

Chapter Thirty-one

Tommy Harp sat on the edge of Kathryn Foreman's king-size bed and tried to wipe the sleep from his eyes. His head was pounding from the many shots of Sambuca the night before. He headed to the bathroom to look for some aspirin in the medicine cabinet. There was a framed photograph on the bathroom wall of Kathryn embracing a man on the stern of a large, Ribovich fishing yacht. The name *Kathryn's Rival* was painted on the transom. The yacht, of course, belonged to James Foreman. But the man in the picture was not the same man who was in the surveillance video in Jackson Hand's office. *What the hell?* He looked again more closely and was sure, it was definitely not the same man. It couldn't have been Kathryn's father because he was much too young. They both looked to be in their early thirties, which would place the time roughly eight years ago. *Kathryn hasn't changed much,* he thought, but there was a weariness that she stoically carried like a badge of honor since the loss of her husband James. *But who the hell is the guy in the photograph?* he wondered. He decided to ask her when he climbed back in bed, "Who's the guy in the picture in the bathroom?"

"My husband, of course," she answered.

"You're kidding. That's James?"

"Yeah. Why does that surprise you?"

"Because I thought I saw a picture of him that looked totally different."

"I've put away most of his pictures since I started seeing you, not that he wouldn't approve. I think James would have liked you, Tommy."

"I'm sure I would have liked him, too."

"So where did you see a picture of James? Was it the one in the library with the silly golf hat?" she asked.

"No, actually, it was at work."

"I don't understand. What do you mean at work?"

"My boss, Jackson Hand, showed me a video tape that caught some guy in an uncompromising position, and he said that it was your late husband."

"That's absurd. James was an impeccably moral person. His only shortcoming was that he was in love with me," she said.

"I'd call that a virtue," said Tommy.

"I was a little naughty for his parent's taste if you know what I mean."

"Stuffed shirts?" asked Tommy.

"The stuffiest, but James was not that way. He had his adventurous side. He just had to temper it because of the responsibilities that he had being a Foreman and an officer in the foundation."

"You're an officer, Kathryn. How come you don't temper your adventurous side?"

"I guess it's because there's no one left alive to disapprove of me. No one that matters, anyway."

"So that's why you can get away with keeping a male bimbo."

"Don't kid yourself, Tommy. You're no bimbo, Honey. If you weren't smart, you'd be late for the door. The sex is nice, but you can't spend your whole life in bed."

"You know, I don't feel that smart. I just took Hand's word for fact that the guy in the video was James."

"What was the uncompromising position," she asked.

"What else, screwing," he said.

"You're not serious?" she demanded. "That bastard!"

"Tell me about it," he said. "The girl in the video was this young black person who he said was a Foreman recipient."

"That may be true, but she certainly wasn't with James."

"That's what I was talking about last night," said Tommy. "When I said I was afraid that a friend was in trouble, I was talking about you."

"Was Hand threatening to blackmail me or possibly the foundation?"

"Not him, but someone. He claimed that he got the tape in the mail."

"Don't believe it for a minute," said Kathryn. She sat up in bed and raked her fingers through her hair. "This is some kind of game of his," she said. "I think James had a run-in with Hand in the past. I seem to remember there was some ugly business about his brother, Evan. Maybe it was Evan that you saw in the video."

"But wouldn't Hand know the difference?" asked Tommy.

"That's exactly my point. He *surely would* know the difference, so he's up to something."

"Should I confront him about it?" asked Tommy.

"Not just yet. Let me talk to Evan first. I think it would be wise to choose just the right time to tip our hands if you know what I mean."

"So, you want me to play along with him?" asked Tommy.

"Well, for the time being, yes. Just act like you're concerned for me and want to protect my precious image."

"I *was* concerned for you, Kathryn, and I *did* want to protect you," he said.

"Oh, Tommy. You're the sweetest bimbo in the whole world," she emoted with her hand across her chest.

"Move that hand, Mrs. Foreman, and I'll show *you* who's sweet."

Chapter Thirty-two

Nellie Brighton and Jay West were having a light lunch when they got the call from Joyce Everly. She told them that they were on the way to the police station to file a complaint against Jackson Hand. Nellie told Joyce that they would meet them there. When she hung up the phone, Jay said to her, "You know, Nellie, this whole thing could blow up in our faces. I'm sure we're guilty of something illegal. Suppression of evidence or *something*."

"Only if someone discovers that we obtained the tapes from Hand's office."

"*I* obtained," said Jay.

"Yes, all right, *you* obtained. Look, we're in this together, Jay. I'm in possession of stolen property, right?"

"You bet your ass, Nellie. I think we're playing with fire here. I say we burn all the shit and be done with it."

"In due time, Jay. Trust me, I know what I'm doing."

"You hope you know what you're doing," said Jay. "Remember, there's a lady across town who's just about a step away from a bottle of pills."

"Don't say that. I'm hoping that Joyce was just being melodramatic."

"See? You're hoping," said Jay West soberly.

~

When they got to the police station, Bill and Joyce Everly were in a conference room with one of the detectives. They asked the desk sergeant to inform them that they were there to support the claim against Jackson Hand.

"Boy, this guy has a lot of friends," the sergeant said sarcastically.

"You can't imagine," said Nellie.

The sergeant ushered them into the room with the Everlys and asked them if they would like anything to drink like water or coffee. They declined and got right down to business.

"If you viewed the tape that Mr. Everly gave you, you'll see that I'm the naked woman that agreed to play along. Mr. Everly has gone to a great deal of trouble to expose this animal."

"I saw the tape," said the detective. "You and Mr. Everly agreed to perform together for the camera?"

"Absolutely. His wife and my boyfriend, Jay, here were well aware of the circumstances. You *have* to put a stop to his extortionist activities."

146

"We'll arrest him, Ms. Brighton," said the detective, "but I can't guarantee a conviction. Basically, it's your word against his. How do you expect the D. A. to prove that he asked you to make the tape? Plus, there wasn't any return address on the envelope that was delivered to Mr. Everly's office. We're dusting the stuff for prints, but I don't think we'll find any."

Jay West produced the cassette tape from his jacket pocket. "I think this will be instrumental in demonstrating the extent of Mr. Hand's involvement."

"An audio tape?" asked the detective.

"Made in Hand's office without his knowledge. Ms. Brighton was aware of the tape and gave her consent, right Nellie?"

"That's right," she said.

"What will I hear on this tape, Ms. Brighton?" he asked.

"You'll hear Hand admitting to having the video tape and sending it to Mr. Everly's office. You'll also hear him implicate himself in a nasty rape for hire scheme involving that poor girl in the theme park."

"Really?" asked the Detective. "My, you people have been very busy, haven't you?"

"Justice never sleeps," said Nellie Brighton.

"If that were the case, I'd be in another line of work," he said. "I'd say it's closer to, *justice sleeps rather poorly!*"

"Well, I know a few people who will sleep much better when that asshole Hand is behind bars," said Joyce Everly.

"You're a remarkable woman, Mrs. Everly. Not many wives would go along with letting their husband get undressed with such a pretty young woman like Ms. Brighton, here," said the detective. Nellie began to blush slightly.

"That man was after my husband, Detective. I intend to do everything in my power to show him that's a very bad idea."

"I'm sure you will, Mrs. Everly. I hope we can put him behind bars for awhile," said the detective.

"A long while," said Nellie Brighton.

Chapter Thirty-three

When Jay West drove Nellie Brighton back to her apartment, they heard the phone ringing just as she was unlocking the door. Her answering machine picked up and she heard the voice of an attorney named Alyssa Shapiro, "Hello Ms. Brighton. This is Alyssa Shapiro with Bunch, Howell and Goldman. Sidney Campbell told me you would be expecting this call. Please call me at your earliest convenience. I think I have some good news for you. My number is area code. . ." Nellie quickly picked up the phone, "Hello. I'm here. I mean, this is Nellie Brighton. My machine picked up, but I'm here."

"Hi, Ms. Brighton. I'm handling your malpractice suit against Brian Sorell. You still want to go through with it, don't you?"

"You bet your ass, I do," said Nellie.

"Good for you. Getting Mr. Sorell disbarred would be a monumental public service, Ms. Brighton."

"Please, call me Nellie," she said.

"And you can call me, Alyssa. We're going to nail this bastard to the cross and he knows it," said Alyssa.

"You've already spoken to him about it?" she asked confused. The wheels of justice seemed to move very fast indeed in the case of Brian Sorell.

"We've been anxious to shut him down for some time, now. Fortunately, he was careless with your case and we think we can prove obstruction. This time we've got him where we want him."

"His carelessness didn't seem too fortunate to me," said Nellie.

"Forgive me, Nellie. That was a poor choice of words. What I mean is that it's fortunate that we have solid evidence of a deliberate criminal activity to present to the grand jury. They'll have no choice but to hold him over for arraignment."

"What does that mean?" asked Nellie.

"It means there will be a trial. He'll be disbarred and go to jail, Nellie. Plus, you'll win an award of at least a million dollars, but probably more like two."

"I just can't believe what I'm hearing," said Nellie with tears filling her eyes.

"Believe it," said Alyssa Shapiro. "He knowingly suppressed evidence that would prove your innocence for personal gain. In light of your recent deposition against Jackson Hand, we feel we can prove a collaboration for the purpose of extortion and blackmail."

"You know about that?" asked Nellie.

"It's public information, Nellie. The computers in our research department cross reference a number of sources by a process called *Data Mining*. Mr. Sorell recommended you for the Job at Jacks and Hands, which led to your forced activities involving Bill and Joyce Everly. It's a rather simple connection, really."

"Will any of the blackmail evidence come to light during this trial?" asked Nellie. She was afraid that her malpractice suit might implicate Joyce Everly as a blackmail victim, which would open up a very dangerous can of worms.

"No, Nellie. It would all be thrown out immediately as inadmissible evidence. None of it is relevant to the basic fact that Mr. Sorell deliberately sabotaged your defense."

"Then, let's do it," said Nellie. "What do you need from me?"

"I need you to turn down his offer," said the attorney.

"What offer," asked Nellie.

"He's going to contact you and tell you that you don't have a case, but that he'll settle out of court to avoid the negative publicity. It'll be a six-figure offer, but it'll also be a joke, about one tenth of what you can expect to be awarded. You'd be foolish to even consider it."

"Don't worry, I won't settle. This is about much more than money," said Nellie.

"Good girl," said 'Alyssa the Hun' as she'd often been called around the water cooler at Bunch, Howell and Goldman. "I want his balls in a Mason jar."

"For your mantle, no doubt?" asked Nellie facetiously.

"For *all our mantles*, Nellie, remember that."

Chapter Thirty-four

When the police arrived at Jackson Hand's office, he was just getting into his car. The two cruisers penned in his shiny new Jaguar with their lights flashing. He stood up and slammed the door saying, "Just what the hell is this?"

"It's called an arrest," said Lieutenant Jeffrey Arnold. He had no idea what a huge favor he was about to do for his wife, Judy. His fishing trip was canceled because of the weather, and he was just doing his job. However, putting Hand behind bars would put an end to the threat of exposure to his wife Judy Arnold and her lover, Joyce Everly.

"What's the charge?" demanded Hand.

"Extortion, with intent to commit blackmail. It has a nice sound to it, doesn't it, Mr. Hand?" chided Officer Arnold.

"You're crazy," he said. "I haven't done anything. Where is your proof?"

"It's not my job to prove anything, Mr. Hand. I just collect the dirt off the street and put it in the can. Right now, you're the number-one turd."

"I'll have your badge for that, Officer Arnold, number 692. Get ready to hit the bricks. I'll bet you'll make a fine security guard."

"I'll send you a soap on a rope, Hand. Get in the car. Feel free to hit your head, as you get in, asshole."

"I pay your salary, Arnold. You can't talk to me like that. You're not related to Judy Arnold, are you?" asked Hand.

"Get in the car, *now!*" said Officer Arnold.

Hand started to laugh and got into the cruiser. The four policemen could hear the automatic locks engage in Hand's Jaguar that he activated with the auto-lock button on his key ring. When he started the car, Jeffrey Arnold's partner, Billy Carl, said, "Ever been to the can, Hand?"

"I need to call my lawyer," he said.

"Want to know who's second on the wish list, almost as popular as child abusers?"

"Fuck you, *officer*," said Hand acidly.

"You guessed it, *blackmailers!*" said Officer Carl, "You're about to make a lot of friends."

Chapter Thirty-five

After receiving a call from Jackson Hand, Brian Sorrell arrived at the police station with a bail bondsman. He walked into the lobby where he was instantly recognized by the sergeant at the desk, "Good afternoon, Mr. Sorrell. Can I interest you in a fresh flea that you can return to the hide of an otherwise proper society?"

"Can it, Riley. You know the drill. I want Hand released in five minutes or else I file for unlawful arrest?"

"Oh, right away, Mr. Sorrell. Gosh gee-willikers. We wouldn't want to piss off a legal giant such as you."

"Just what is your problem, Riley?" asked Sorrell. "You give me shit every time I come in here."

"Let's just say I don't like the caliber of your clientele."

"Everybody deserves a good defense," said Sorrell.

"Not everybody," said Riley. "Some of them deserve you."

Chapter Thirty-six

Hand was escorted to the front lobby of the police precinct by a very large, African American officer who released him from his handcuffs and said, "You're free to go, Mr. Hand."

"Hello, Brian," said Hand. "Have you reviewed the charges?"

"Briefly, Jackson. I haven't had a chance to read all the depositions yet."

"Well, what am I paying you for, dammit? *Read the damned things.*"

"Take it easy, Jackson. We'll get it straightened out. Just remain calm, okay?"

"You remain calm, Brian. I was just in jail," he fumed. "Just how serious are the charges?"

"It's a felony if it sticks. You'd have to do time."

"That's not an option, counselor. It better not stick or it'll stick to you, too. Do I make myself clear?"

"*Jesus,*" said Sorell. "Would you keep your voice down. At least until we get in the car."

"Where's *my* car," demanded Hand.

"It's in the impound. We'll get it back tomorrow."

"There better not be a scratch on it," said Hand viciously.

"I think right about now that's the least of your problems," said Brian Sorell.

Chapter Thirty-seven

Out on the street there were four Jacks and two Hands lounging on Brian Sorell's Mercedes Benz. One Hand in particular was sitting on the hood and grinding the leather heel of her boot forward and back producing ugly scratches in the paint.

"What the hell do you think you're doing," screamed Sorell to the woman on his car.

"Do you remember me, Mr. Sorell? You were my lawyer about two years ago. I spent six months in prison for a jewelry store robbery. The stolen jewels were found in my apartment. Sound familiar? Then you sold my soul to Mr. Hand. I was innocent as you well know. Well, there's something that you don't know. That was the end of my innocence. I've recovered the surveillance tape that showed me breaking into Mr. Hand's condo. What it didn't show was that I was acting under his orders to supposedly test his new security system. If he turned over the tape, it was back to prison. I've been under his thumb ever since until today when I received and destroyed the evidence. Jay West was nice enough to give it to me. There's nothing that you, or your evil little troll of a cohort can do to me now, so I just thought I'd do a little decorating on the hood of your car. Do you like it?"

"I remember you, Sandra," said Sorell. "You can't just damage someone else's property and not expect to be held responsible."

"I suppose you're right. From now on, I am going to be responsible. I hereby take responsibility for your life."

Sandra Foley then looked Brian Sorell straight in the eye and held her hand out-stretched in his direction just slightly over her head. She then closed her fist and extended her thumb and curled it toward the pavement ending in a thumbs-down gesture. The symbolism was not lost on Sorell.

One of the Jacks then spoke up, "We will all take responsibility for your lives." His name was Curtis Meyers, and he was held hostage for the last three years in Jackson Hand's cruel stable.

His crime was one of passion in that he killed the Jack that Hand had ordered to photograph his sister during a drunken, drug induced stupor. The difference being that the murder weapon was retrieved by Jay West and returned to him rather than being held by a particular police evidence room as in the case of Sam Weller.

He believed that the killing was justified, but the point was moot. He had disposed of the weapon that implicated him just as Sandra Foley had disposed of her tape. In fact,

Jay west had delivered all ten damning pieces of evidence to the Jacks and Hands that Jackson Hand had under his control for his stable.

The only tape that Jackson Hand still had in his office was the one that featured Kathryn Forman's brother-in-law, Evan with the pretty, young African-American recipient of a Forman Foundation scholarship. When Jay West asked Tommy Harp if Jackson Hand was blackmailing him, Jay was told of the tape and promised to recover it for Evan Foreman. Jay took that opportunity to talk to Mr. Foreman about a possible "favor" in return. If all went according to plan, the Jacks and Hands would need the services of a good attorney such as Evan Foreman.

Jackson Hand and Brian Sorell knew that the smartest thing to do would be to put as much distance between themselves and the Jacks and Hands as possible. Unfortunately, that realization came a little too late. The Jacks then rushed forward with impossible speed. Their cries were quickly muffled by gags in their mouths and strips of cloth securing them tied around the back of their heads. Such a daring attempt of a broad daylight abduction would have been unthinkable were it not for the additional two Jacks and three Hands securing the perimeter.

There were three possible witnesses, but in each case, a diversion was executed perfectly. Two Jacks and one Hand stepped into place and caught the attention of the witnesses to avoid any possible detection. They reasoned that if the abduction didn't come off smoothly, they could abort the mission and resume at some further time of their choosing. There would be no escape. Time was finally on their side.

Chapter Thirty-eight

The yacht that was James Forman's favorite toy was seventy-two feet of custom sport fishing perfection. It had mahogany planking guaranteed to raise any self-respecting school of dolphin with the finely tuned resonance she created at a trolling speed of six to eight knots. The boat builder's name on the side of the hull was *Ribovich,* and the name on the transome was *Kathryn's Rival.* All the appointments within its spacious interior were done in precious hardwoods such as teak, ebony and jacaranda. It was every trim carpenter's dream to apply his art to the interior of a beauty like *Kathryn's Rival.*

The yacht was owned by the late James Foreman who was the founder and CEO of the Foreman Foundation. After his passing, James' wife, Kathryn, decided to keep the beautiful yacht because it continued to remind her of so many good times they shared while onboard. Ever since she met Tommy Harp and became his lover, she was considering letting go of the physical things that bound her to the memory of James. Material possessions were never foremost on Kathryn's list of priorities, so when her brother-in-law, Evan Foreman, approached her about the prospect of borrowing the yacht, he found her surprisingly receptive to the idea.

Jay West and Nellie Brighton had delivered the original copy of the Foreman blackmail tape that Jackson Hand showed Tommy Harp in his office. It was among the tapes and physical evidence taken from Jackson Hand's safe. Although a copy of the Foreman tape was still in the VCR in Jackson Hand's office, Evan was assured by Jay West that it was only a matter of time before he would have it in his hand.

Evan was hoping that he would be able to return the magnificent fishing yacht without the stain of any tragic incidence, but he knew the plan of the Jacks and Hands and stood firmly behind it. When he first learned of the tape, which compromised his position and suitability as a board member of the Forman Foundation, he was furious. Furthermore, when he learned that Jackson Hand intended to harm not only him but his grieving sister-in-law, he could barely control the murderous rage that seemed to boil the blood coursing through his veins.

As an attorney himself, Evan Foreman knew that Jackson Hand could very well beat the charges and escape with nothing more than a slap on the wrist. Brian Sorell, of whom he was familiar and sorely contemptuous of, had already gotten him out on bail. Evan was anxious to help the Jacks and Hands put a stop to Jackson Hand's extortionist activities by any means short of murder. However, he was prepared to leave the yacht if necessary in order to look the other way. In the mean time, his considerable talents in corporate law would serve the Jacks and Hands very well indeed during the long night ahead of them. Jackson Hand and Brian Sorell were to be reluctant guests aboard *Kathryn's Rival* for an evening of intense negotiations - resulting in the hostile takeover of the company known as *Jacks and Hands.*

The Jacks and Hands that made up Hand's *stable* were all present aboard the yacht except for Sam Weller. Unfortunately, Jay West was not able to produce the incriminating evidence against him. The gun with his fingerprints still sat, in silent accusation in the evidence room of the Coconut Grove Police Department. However, all the other Jacks and Hands that had been under Jackson Hand's despicable power were there at hand to exact their vengeance. Evan Foreman made it an even dozen.

They were seven Hands, four Jacks and a corporate attorney. A full complement of corporate raiders headed for the Gulf Stream with two hostile adversaries tied up neatly and gagged in the galley. Tommy Harp and Sam Weller were in another boat called *Foreplay,* which was owned by Evan Foreman. It was a thirty-nine-foot Sea Ray that was set up more for comfort than fishing. The basic plan was to rendezvous at a location called Bethel Shoal and raft-up the two vessels for *"negotiations"* with Jackson Hand and Brian Sorell.

Chapter Thirty-nine

*K*athryn's *Rival* reached Bethel Shoal well ahead of *Foreplay*. Jay West and Nellie Brighton were seated on a comfortable bench-seat atop the flying bridge. The captain's chair was a short distance in front of them where Evan Foreman was looking over the SAT-NAV readout.

"You think Tommy Harp will be able to find us in the middle of all this water?" asked Jay.

"Shouldn't be a problem," said Evan. "I radioed the SAT-NAV numbers. That'll narrow us down to within fifty feet."

Nellie Brighton couldn't believe how helpful Evan Foreman and the Everlys were being in bringing Jackson Hand down. Everyone seemed to understand the huge importance of the task. Nellie asked Jay, "Do you think Hand will turn over the company to the Jacks and Hands?"

"He better," said Jay.

"Is it legal?" she asked Evan.

"Absolutely. Anyone can purchase a company, even in the middle of the Atlantic Ocean," said Evan. "We've even got his lawyer to witness the transaction."

"What if Hand claims the deal was made under duress?" asked Nellie.

"If he survives this night, I'm sure he won't want anything to do with Jacks and Hands anymore," said Jay. "There are at least a dozen people who have every reason to make his life a living hell. When he realizes that all of his dirty leverage is gone, he'll freak, believe me. He'll be incredibly vulnerable for the first time, and it'll shake his reality to the core. I doubt if he'll remain in North America."

"What do you mean *if* he survives," said Nellie clearly irritated. "I'm not going to be a part of any murder, Jay. We were clear on that, right?"

"Calm down, Nellie. Neither am I. I can't speak for the other Jacks and Hands, though. They're assembled like a war party in the galley."

"What about Hand and Sorell," asked Even. "They still out?"

"I think so," said Jay. "I asked Phil Cooper to let us know when they come around."

"Somebody call my name?" asked Cooper climbing the stairs to the wheelhouse. *"It's showtime!"* he said, meaning that the time was finally at hand when the Jacks and Hands would be compensated for all of their suffering.

"We can't be witness to anything ugly, Phil. Does everybody understand that?" asked Jay.

"We're all in agreement," he said. "If we can't reach a meeting of the minds, so to speak, the three of you go aboard *Foreplay* and head back ahead of us with Tommy Harp and that asshole, Sorell. Then we rendezvous just outside the inlet and exchange boats. No questions asked, right?"

"Right as rain," said Evan, "but I hope it doesn't have to come to that."

"I don't care either way," said Cooper.

"Does he know?" asked Jay.

"Does who know what?" asked Cooper.

"Does Hand know I emptied his safe?"

"We thought you'd like to tell him yourself."

"Thanks."

Chapter Forty

J ay and Nellie followed Phil Cooper down the stairs and through the spacious cabin to the galley of *Kathryn's Rival*. There they joined the two other Jacks and six Hands that made up the stable. Jackson Hand and Brian Sorell were seated at a table rubbing their temples, just coming awake. They each had sizeable headaches. When Hand saw Jay West, he asked, "Just what the hell's going on here, West?"

"It's your worst nightmare, Hand. Yours, too, Sorell."

"You're all in a lot of trouble," said Sorell, "You know that, don't you?"

"What makes you say that?" asked Jay.

"Kidnapping? Are you kidding me?" asked Hand. "But I have other ways of punishing you all, and you know it."

"You have nothing," said Jay.

"I left instructions and arrangements for the police to examine the contents of my safe. You're all screwed."

"Your safe is empty, Hand," said Jay. "I emptied it."

"I doubt that," said Hand.

"Have you been able to open it lately?" he asked.

"I can get it open, and when I do. . ."

169

"You'll find it empty. I can give you the combination. I changed it."

"Changed it? How?"

"I found it unlocked and emptied it. Then I changed the combination. It's very simple when the door is open," said Jay.

"When did you supposedly have access to my office," asked Hand.

"Yesterday, when Susan had her car keyed, and Nellie had her little breakdown at the front desk of your office complex. I returned all the evidence to the respective victims. You now have zero leverage, zero power and many, many enemies. Just what do you think your chances are of getting off this boat alive?"

Jackson Hand started to perspire heavily. The message was starting to sink in.

"Just what the hell's going on here," demanded Sorell.

"You ever wonder how you were gonna' die, Jackson?" asked Phil Cooper.

"Oh, my God," said Jackson Hand starting to shake visibly.

"Oh, relax, Jackson," said Sorell. "They can't kill us. I take it that we're aboard some kind of boat," he began, "and someone must be piloting the boat, therefore, witnesses. No, I don't think they want to go to jail for conspiracy to commit murder."

"There will be no witness, Sorell, but all that will become clear to you in a short while. What we have to discuss now is how much you would like to avoid getting in the water with a cinder block chained to your leg."

"You're all insane," said Hand. His hands were shaking badly.

"Yes, we are," said Cooper. "And you made us this way. Even if you meet our demands, there are some people in this room who won't sleep very well knowing that you're still alive somewhere. Therefore, I recommend a change in residence as soon as possible."

"Demands? What demands?" asked Hand.

"We want the company," spoke up Nellie. "Joint ownership for the twelve Jacks and Hands of the stable."

"You're crazy," said hand.

"That's not all, Hand," said Cooper. "We know about your offshore bank accounts in the Cayman Islands. We want four million dollars transferred to an account that we have set up. We'll then pay you back one million for the company."

"Like I said, you're all crazy," said Hand.

"And you're dead," said Cooper.

Chapter Forty-one

The Gulf Stream is just as beautiful at night as it is in the middle of the day. The moonlight cascades down through the water and dissipates in moving shafts of sapphire, folding in on itself on the rise and fall of the rolling swells. The mood would have been romantic were it not for the grisly task at hand.

It was a mood that could be shattered by a scream in the night or embraced after the successful conclusion of the Jacks and Hands' hostile takeover of the company. The night would deal a new hand of cards to a dozen people, cards that would play out for years to come in the form of regrets or boastful victories. Nellie Brighton was throwing up over the railing of the massive sport-fisherman. Only she knew for sure that it was not the result of seasickness.

When Hand and Sorell arrived on deck, Phil Cooper began to lay the ground work for the negotiations, "Here's what we expect to have happen, Hand. All of the Jacks and Hands on this boat were a part of your stable. There are eleven of us here in all. The only missing member is Sam Weller, but he'll be along shortly. You will sign over all rights to the company known *as Jacks and Hands* to the twelve of us. We all are to have equal shares of the company.

Furthermore, we have learned from our captain, who is also our attorney by the way, that your bank account in the Cayman Islands exceeds five million dollars. We expect you to wire four million dollars to an account also held jointly by the twelve of us.

It seems the Foreman Foundation does a considerable amount of business with the Banque de Cayman and has been kind enough to arrange the transfer of funds at a moment's notice, any time of the day or night. An account executive is standing by. Do you understand?"

"Go to hell," said Jackson Hand.

Just then, one of the Jacks called out, "Here they come!"

Nellie looked toward the eastern horizon and saw Evan Forman's boat, *Foreplay,* bearing down on them. After about ten minutes they cut the throttles and drifted up near *Kathryn's Rival.*

At the helm was Tommy Harp and manning the ropes to raft-up was Sam Weller.

Tommy brought the sleek Sea Ray alongside the huge Ribovich and called out, "Ahoy, *Kathryn's Rival.* Permission to raft-up, Captain?"

"Permission granted," said Evan Foreman. Evan then left the wheelhouse of *Kathryn's Rival* and made his way down the stairs and along the rail toward *Foreplay.* Two Jacks escorted Brian Sorell along the rail to Evan's boat as well. After Evan and Sorell transferred to *Foreplay*, Jay West spoke up for the first time, "Last chance, Hand. There go your witnesses, and Nellie and I are just about to join them."

Sam Weller came aboard *Kathryn's Rival* and said, "Hello, Jackson. Nice night for a swim, don't you think?"

"Fuck you, Weller," said Hand.

"You already have, Jackson. Now, it's my turn. I got the letter from your safe, which was addressed to the Coconut Grove Police Department. Plus, Mr. Foreman assures me that if you ever make the call, you only implicate yourself by virtue of an audio tape that Jay West furnished to the police. Your cards are all spent, Jackson. All you have left is a shitty hand."

Jay West and Nellie Brighton were to be the last to leave *Kathryn's Rival*. Tommy Harp started *Foreplay's* engines and gave the order to cast off. Phil Cooper told Tommy Harp he would radio him to raft-up again when they were through with the *negotiations*.

They were leaving Jackson Hand and ten stable members behind. Four Jacks and six Hands would try to convince Jackson Hand that he would be better off leaving the country with the two million dollars they would leave in his Cayman Island account.

Chapter Forty-two

Dangling from the outrigger there were lanterns that cast a dingy yellow light on the surface of the water. The Jacks were emptying buckets of chopped-up fish and cow's blood into the sea. It was only a matter of time before the sharks would appear. Phil Cooper and Melissa Coolidge, a tall muscular blond Hand, were putting large chunks of bloody chicken on double-ought hooks.

Melissa had been drugged with *roofies* on Jackson Hand's orders and became an unwitting member of a photographed orgy. Her father had a very delicate heart condition and was subject to coronaries at the drop of a hat. Jackson Hand often delighted in handing her an envelope addressed to her father and asking, "Here, Melissa, would you please drop this in the mailbox for me?" Melissa would tear open the envelope, then tear up the photographs and routinely burst into tears. She was smiling now hoping for the slim chance that she could witness the sharks tearing into Jackson Hand's flesh. When Jay West delivered the photographs, complete with the negatives, to her, she was the one who suggested the night of shark fishing.

Apparently, she had been having the perverse fantasy for some time.

At first there were only blue sharks responding to the chum line. They began to circle the boat in a lazy dance, bumping one another slowly at first, and then slashing with their tails as they darted quickly forward. Most of the sharks were only four to five feet in length, but their numbers were increasing rapidly in what would surely end up as a feeding frenzy. Cooper then gave the order to, "Cuff him to the chain." Hand was sure all the drama was just for show. He was wrong.

One of the Jacks then came forward with a three-foot coil of one-inch rubber coated chain. A hand snapped one of the cuffs through the end link in the chain and then snapped the other cuff over Jackson Hand's left wrist. The chain was attached to the end of a 200-pound-test line filling a power winch bolted to the transom. Hand watched them go through the motions and was very impressed by their determination to make the situation seem as real as possible. He was wrong.

Cooper gave the order, "Throw him over the side!"

Two Jacks picked up Hand who then started to squirm and say, "Cut it out. You know you're not actually going to throw me over the siiiiide!" He was wrong.

Hand's body hit the water with a loud splash, and the boat moved off and began to pay out the line.

Melissa Coolidge began to smile again as did more than a few of the other Jacks and Hands.

Chapter Forty-three

Aboard *Foreplay*, Brian Sorell was asking Evan Foreman, "Do you really think you can get away with this fiasco?"

I've agreed to captain my sister-in-law's boat for a fishing party and business meeting between Jackson Hand and his employees. Do you see something sinister in that?"

"You're aiding and abetting kidnapers for God's sake," said Sorell furiously.

"That's your point of view, Mr. Sorell. I've seen nothing that can be construed as an illegal act. I have only your word that there has actually been an abduction of any sorts. How would I ever know that you weren't a willing participant of this charter? That makes you a co-conspirator as well, doesn't it?"

"It won't wash, Mr. Foreman. And if Mr. Hand is killed by the maniacs on that other boat, you'll be guilty of conspiracy to commit murder."

"Oh, I hardly think so," said Evan. "However, I couldn't care less what actually happens to the bastard. You shouldn't either, Mr. Sorell. He'll do nothing but take you down with him, and make no mistake about it, he's headed for a fall."

"Be that as it may, counselor, I'm sure you realize that any transaction executed in the middle of shark fishing adventure is not exactly binding by the courts."

"I have no idea what you're talking about. The purchase of a company can take place at any time and at any place acceptable to the parties involved. I'm sure when we rejoin the other boat, Mr. Hand will be a willing participant to the transfer of assets.

You, Mr. Sorell are only required to witness the transaction. If you refuse, then I presume Mr. Hand will need another attorney. In either case, you are Mr. Hand's employee. He has retained your services to act as his attorney. Why don't we wait and see what his wishes are before you presume to decide the legality of the matter, shall we?"

"By all means, counselor. Play out your little sick game," said Sorell.

"Speaking of games," said Nellie Brighton, "I know an attorney named Alyssa Shapiro who's anxious to play a game called *put the balls in the Mason jar*. Doesn't that sound like fun, Mr. Sorell?"

Chapter Forty-four

J ackson Hand's screams could be heard clearly from a hundred yards away. The first blue had brushed along side him, testing his flight response ability. Hand had no ability to flee, so he screamed loud and long. The Jacks and Hands in the boat responded by reeling him forward toward *Kathryn's Rival*. Although they pulled him forward rather quickly, the time seemed like an eternity to Jackson Hand. He had the presence of mind to grab hold of the chain with his left hand instead of letting himself be pulled along by the handcuff cutting into his wrist.

However, each agonizing minute was fraught with the expectation of a sudden pain accompanied by a pulling feeling as a shark took one of his extremities away from him. As he neared the transom of *Kathryn's Rival*, he screamed at the Jacks and Hands, "Pull me aboard! Pull me aboard! I'll agree to whatever you want!"

It was music to the ears of the former stable. They knew that their future was crystallizing, and that Jackson Hand was finished.

The Jacks and Hands were drunk with the sense of their accomplishment. Jay West had become their deliverer, and he would be exalted for the rest of his life. If he had decided to form a religion at that very moment, he would have had ten very devout followers in the blink of an eye.

However, Jay West wasn't interested in followers. He wasn't even interested in his percentage of the company. All he wanted was Nellie Brighton and a chance to start over away from Jacks and Hands.

When they pulled Jackson Hand aboard *Kathryn's Rival,* he was in shock. His body was still intact, but his mind might never be the same again. He had a high fever, and a greasy sweat broke out on his forehead. He wasn't quite coherent, but he kept muttering, over and over, "Whatever you want - whatever you want."

Phil Cooper raised *Foreplay* on the radio and gave them the signal that the deal was done. The power play was over. Jackson Hand would gratefully pick up whatever pieces the stable left to him and move on. He would ask Brian Sorell to cooperate fully with the wishes of the stable. He was done.

The business of transferring the company was to resume as soon as *Foreplay* rafted up again with *Kathryn's Rival.* Sorell was needed as a witness, and Evan Foreman was needed to represent the Jacks and Hands.

Phil Cooper decided to help matters by closing the distance between the two boats at three quarter's speed.

Twenty minutes later, the two boats rafted-up once again over Thomas Shoal in two hundred sixty feet of water. The Banque de Cayman was contacted and Jackson Hand managed to transfer four million dollars to the joint account of the stable. Then the deal was struck to sell the business of Jacks and Hands to the stable members for one million dollars. The purchase price was to be transferred state-side to Jackson Hand's brokerage account at Charles Schwab first thing in the morning.

It was done. The Jacks and Hands, who were once the stable, now owned the company. The other twelve (non-stable) Jacks and Hands would never know the difference except for Tommy Harp. He was never really caught up in the dirty business of the Jacks and Hands *stable* but was an instrumental part of their deliverance. He continued to work for the company oblivious to the change in ownership; however, he resigned ten days later when Kathryn Foreman asked him to marry her. He said, "Yes."

Brian Sorell threatened to challenge the sale of Jacks and Hands on the grounds that it was made under extreme duress. Nellie Brighton, once again, came to the rescue by agreeing to settle her malpractice law suit against him out of court for nine hundred thousand dollars, with the proviso that he turns states evidence against Jackson Hand.

~

Joyce Everly and Judy Arnold remain lovers and are happier than they have been in quite some time.

~

Evan Foreman renewed his relationship with his young African-American friend.

~

Phil Cooper was elected Chairman of the Board of Jacks and Hands, and Sam Weller was elected vice chairman.

~

Jay West and Nellie Brighton remain absentee owners of their shares of the company from St. Thomas in the U.S. Virgin Islands. They have a young son who excels at soccer.

~

Brian Sorell remains Brian Sorell. It is not a perfect world.

~

Jackson Hand is taking great pains to be someone else, somewhere else, or someone out of time. Many Jacks and Hands would enjoy traveling to a very remote island off the coast of Mauritius called Rodrigues. There they might discover that along with the *Ramus Mania,* which is the rarest wild coffee plant in the world, they could also find the Rodrigues fruit bat and a very lonely fisherman who was once known as Jackson Hand.

JACKS & HANDS